In 2017 Tommy Swerdlow directed, co-wrote, and co-starred in a movie called *A Thousand Junkies*. It boils addiction down to one work day for three addicts, as they drive all over Los Angeles trying to get what they need. In many ways *Straight Dope* is a companion piece for that movie—another dark love letter to L.A. drawing on Swerdlow's thirty-seven years making trouble, and writing movies here.

Here's what the critics had to say about *A Thousand Junkies*...

"Simultaneously absurd, playful, and horrific."
—John Fink, *The Film Stage*

"*A Thousand Junkies* is that rare film to expertly balance lunacy with pathos, dread and light-heartedness."
—Nathanael Hood, *Audiences Everywhere*

"Telling the story of three heroin addicts trying to find a fix in L.A., *A Thousand Junkies* is a fast-paced and deliciously dark black comedy, which (unsurprisingly) oozes authenticity."
—*Film Daily*

"The problem is that, as anyone who has spent time with junkies knows, they're not a terribly interesting lot. To its credit, the film's depiction of its characters always feels truthful."
—Frank Scheck, *The Hollywood Reporter*

"The feature directorial debut of screenwriter Tommy Swerdlow, *A Thousand Junkies* strikes a nerve and strikes a delicate tonal balance, often making the viewer laugh and cringe from painful identification within a matter of seconds."
—Matt Grobar, *Deadline Hollywood*

Straight Dope

Tommy Swerdlow

Stark House Press • Eureka California

STRAIGHT DOPE

Published by Stark House Press
1315 H Street
Eureka, CA 95501, USA
griffinskye3@sbcglobal.net
www.starkhousepress.com

ISBN-13: 978-1-951473-37-2

Book design by Mark Shepard, shepgraphics.com
Cover art by John di Mena

First Stark House Press Edition: July 2021

This book would not have made it home without the help of Deirdre Lewis, Veronica Shulman, Chani Krich, Karen Swerdlow and my friends at Document coffee in Koreatown where much of it was written.

1.

For years the forecast had been "No." No and windy, no and cloudy, no with a chance of showers. At times, it seemed the sun might break through, but it was always a hoax, and even when it did it was that harsh, flat, smog-sick light that blasts you out, and breaks you down to nothing. Los Angeles isn't for people. It's for lizards. Human beings weigh too much for this town, and the ground breaks away from under their feet. Some folks don't like that feeling, and lurch to get their balance, but some have learned to love it, and believe their footsteps actually change the shape of the earth. New York is different—it's built on granite and good taste, but L.A. is made of crumbling clay and whatever you can get away with, and for awhile, I got away with it all.

But then the weather changed, and the barometric pressure grabbed me by the throat. I needed it to rain, but all it did was blow, a steady and relentless gale of "no" coming off the ocean and tearing down Wilshire Boulevard.

#

I just arrived at the fancy artisan coffee shop, one of thirty in a half-mile radius. I can't pay my rent, but I can afford a six-dollar cup of coffee. That's an L.A. mindset if ever there was one. Actors and writers live like they're rich, 'cause when they get paid they get paid a lot, but for most those paydays are few and far between. For a long time I was one of the lucky. Now I'm one of the most. I look out at the world from my little sidewalk perch on Larchmont. I see banks I got no money in, people I can't relate to, and real estate brokers with houses I can't afford, but for some reason I still got a goofy smile on my face. I reach for my little science beaker of "Costa Rica" when my phone starts to rattle on the table like a piece of bacon frying. It's not even eight yet, so it's either a bill collector or my ex-wife needing me to take Stanley to school, but the screen says "Angie English." I was not expecting that.

— Something tells me this is a butt dial?

Silence. I am both relieved and disappointed.

— Is that how you answer the phone these days, sweetie?

So, she had meant to call.

— Not usually. Just not expecting to hear from you, and definitely not at 7:30 in the morning.

— I'm sorry, is it too early? You're usually up half six, aren't you?

— I was up before half six. I was up whole six.

She fake-laughed, but it was a real fake laugh.

— How've you been, sweetie?

— Sweetie's been good. How's Miss Angie?

— I haven't had my coffee yet, so I don't really know.

— Yeah, just having mine now. You in America?

— Yes, if I wasn't, I'd be Skyping, and you wouldn't be answering because you still don't know how to set your alert.

There's something about a classy, female British accent in the morning that really clears the sinuses.

— What are you doing, sweetie?

— Why, you want to drag me up Runyon Canyon and show me how much better shape you're in than me?

When we had met I was about six months off my "medication," and three years off open-heart surgery, and for our first date, she had proposed a hike. After five minutes of steep uphill travel, I was doubled over on a bench trying to remember my name. She looked down at me and said, "We have to get you in proper shape, sweetie, you've things to do." I looked up at her, a glowing swan of colonial goodness, and thought to myself, "Finally, a woman who will guide me to the light."

— Do you have anything this morning? I need to talk to you, and it's a bit on the pressing side.

The lilting tea-and-scones flirtation was gone.

— Why, what is it?

— I'd rather not over the phone.

— Well you got to give me some idea or I'm going to think I've done something wrong.

— Why would you think that?

— 'Cause I usually have.

She gave a chuckle. That one was real.

— Could you come up to Malibu? I don't feel like going anywhere, and it's the kind thing that needs to be discussed in person. Besides, it's lovely up here today, the wind's blown everything out, and the sky is glorious, and I know Chagall would love to see you ... Come now, and I'll make you a juice.

Chagall was her dog, though it was a better name for a cat.

— Please, it's a difficult time, and it's just one of those mornings where I don't want to come into town, so please, just come, it really is breathtaking up here this morning. We can chat, take a walk on that sweet little trail through the scrub, and then go down to that little shack for fish-and-chips. Please, Bobby, I very much need to talk to you.

She was speaking in fast unending breaths like she couldn't get rid of the words quick enough.

— Talk to me about what?

— Not over the phone. Just come to the house, can you come now?

— I have a call at ten.

— What kind of call?

— Business. Movie shit.

— Oh really, how's that all going anyway?

— I'll tell you after the call.

— Well, why don't you get in the car and beat the traffic and you can make the call from here.

— I don't get reception up there.

— You can use my landline. I can give you some breakfast if you haven't eaten.

— Kippers and eggs?

— You are obsessed with kippers and eggs.

I laughed and released a little tension.

— Please, just come now. There could be some money in it for you. Real money. Not a huge sum, but an amount. I know you could use some money, couldn't you?

My pause answered that one.

— Please, sweetie. Do this for me. Just come.

Well, at least we were back to sweetie.

2.

I'm on the 10 just before it becomes the PCH and I'm headed
north to Malibu. This part of the 10 has been designated as the
Rosa Parks Freeway, which is kind of funny because I haven't seen
a black driver since LaBrea, and I probably won't the rest of the
way. The phone rings as I pass the Getty villa. It's lying face-down
on the passenger seat, and I take one hand off the wheel in the
middle of a blind curve to flip it over. It's a 424 area code so it's
either showbiz calling or the Century City dentist I owe eleven
grand to. I decide to live dangerously and answer.
— Hello.
— Hi, Bobby, it's Colleen at Suspicious.
Suspicious Entertainment was a production company that I was
working with on a pitch. They were flying high after a huge
animated hit based on an iconic toy line.
— Andrew has to meet with Ray at ten, and he was wondering if
you can do the call now?
Ray was the founder, a Korean whiz kid who looked like a Mafia
don and had broken down the door remaking Asian films for
American audiences.
— Now, like right this minute?
She laughed. It was another real fake laugh. I was getting a lot
of them this morning.
— If you can, or we can call you back in five if you need a moment.
It's just Andrew's schedule is packed today, and I know he wants
to talk to you.
— Okay.
— Do you need a minute?
— No, I'm good. Is Nick going to be on the call?
— He will, I'm getting him now, he's in his car.
Nick was under Andrew, but a smart kid. And by smart, I mean
he listened more than he talked. Andrew on the other hand, was
a loose can who, like so many others, had figured out a way to turn
a near terminal case of ADD into as thriving Hollywood career."
Lose "like so many others" so it reads "had learned to turn a near
terminal case of ADD into a thriving Hollywood career. I had met
him a couple of months back on a "general meeting" over at the

Warner Brothers lot. His bipolar disorder was working for him that morning, and within five minutes it was established that we were both "friends of Bill," which meant we were both in AA. Once he realized he was with a fellow disaster, he just let it rip, his thoughts bouncing like a super ball off the movie-postered walls.

After a fifteen minute rant covering addiction, childhood, donuts, and poetry, he finally came up for air. Then he leaned forward and cocked an eyebrow. "I loved *Freetown*. I fucking loved it, dude." *Freetown* was a script I had written about a kid in civil-war-torn Sierra Leone who makes his way to America. "I've got this idea. It's incredible, but I can't crack it. I've been trying and trying and I'm all around it, but I just can't crack it." Then he looked at me like I knew something he didn't, and said, "But maybe you can." He sat down cross-legged on the floor and told me the crux of his magic idea. Ten minutes later it was "our" magic idea, and Andrew Wood and I were in business. But now it was three months later, and I had yet to see a dime.

— Hey, dude. Thanks for moving the call up.

— No problem. Is Nick on?

— Here dude.

— Talked to DreamWorks yesterday, they're excited to hear. You got to go in and crush this thing. DreamWorks is the perfect place for it.

Two weeks ago, he had said it didn't feel like a DreamWorks project. Truth was, it didn't matter. There were only a few places that made one-hundred-million-dollar cartoons, and we'd been to all of them. Each one had said how much they loved it, then passed. DreamWorks was the only place left.

— You know Dennis Destitrino over there, he thought he might have worked with you, but wasn't sure.

— The only person I know over there is Jeffrey.

I said that to let them know that I was too artistic to keep tabs on development executives, and that the only person I did know over there was the man who cofounded and ran the company, one Jeffrey Katzenberg, because I was the original (and uncredited) writer on the very first *Shrek*, a movie I felt I had made a huge contribution to and had been waiting twenty years to be acknowledged for. And by acknowledged, I mean hired for another gig.

— Dude, I'm not sure about the Puff the Magic Dragon beat, at least for the pitch. It's funny, but we have other funny stuff, and I think we're a little long.

— Really? I like it.

That was Nick. He was taking Wood on, right off the bat.

— I like it too, but we're long. I don't want to be long, don't get me wrong, you tell it great (that was to me), but last time it was almost thirty-five, and twenty to twenty-five is all they can take if they can take that.

If anyone knew about short attention spans, it was Wood. But Nick wasn't giving up easy.

— It's gotten a laugh every time, dude.

— So has Buffalo Soldier with his dreadlocks smoking weed.

— I don't think we should cut a dependable big laugh.

— It didn't get a big laugh at Paramount.

— That's true, it got a chuckle at Paramount, but it got a big laugh at Sony and Buffalo Soldier fell flat.

— It's different every time.

That was me.

— That's the nature of the beast. You can't pencil in the laughs. Besides, the woman at Fox barely cracked a smile the whole time and she liked it more than anyone. I mean, we can definitely lose it, it's not essential story, we just have to go from Black Magic Woman's cabin, to climbing Ain't No Mountain High Enough, meet the Fool On The Hill, hear about Major Tom, and then we just go right to the Disco Queen's queendom without getting picked up by Puff in the Volkswagen bus.

If you had heard me speaking out of context I would have sounded like a mental patient in mid-episode, but this is what I had spent my entire adult life doing. Talking about ridiculous, intricate, and imaginary circumstances like they were absolutely real. It was what six-year-olds did. The only difference was I got paid good money to do it, or at least, I used to. Anyway, whether we cut Puff or kept him in, we were down to the wire, and now we just had one bullet left, one last flare to fire out into the Hollywood darkness, one final chance to kneel prostrate before the pitch gods and say, "Love us, please, love us and our little puppet show enough to write a decent start-up check for the script and then who knows, maybe you'll give us ninety mil to make the movie. And I'll be back in the game."

3.

I stand out on her street and ring the bell. Across the street is a house with a Shetland pony in the front yard. Fucking Malibu. She opens the door dressed in a teal satin kimono, and looks at me like I'm a FedEx package she's been waiting for all morning.

— What time's your business call?

— Already happened, they had to move it up.

— That was fortunate; go well?

— It was completely unnecessary, so I guess it went great.

Her auburn hair was in a Bonnie and Clyde bob and set off by the English countryside cheekbones.

— I don't understand your business at all.

— That makes two of us.

— It's backward as an arse in front.

— Yeah, and the art world makes so much sense.

She owned a gallery in Santa Monica. Or maybe she had sold it.

We're standing in her whitewashed stucco courtyard with the multicolored bougainvillea growing perfectly up the walls and onto the terra-cotta roof. We could have been in Mallorca or Corfu. I guess that was the point. I look over at her little shrine area with the three Buddhas and the Hindu deity I always forget the name of. Just what the world needs, more privileged, white Anglos aping other cultures' gods because they can't come up with any good ones of their own.

— Are you taking care of yourself?

— I am ... At least in that way.

— You're very lucky to be alive, Bobby.

I gave her a smile I couldn't understand the meaning of in a million years, then glanced down at her feet. They were tan and arched and ridiculously bare, and I was flooded with a quick, savage desire to fuck that I could taste in my mouth like a steak. A huge gust blew up, sending the trees into a frenzy, their silver-green leaves flashing in the sunlight like a school of anchovies swimming in the sky.

— Let's go inside, Sweetie, this wind can you make mad.

#

— Where's Chagall?
— He's out back on the hill. He's become enraptured with the squirrels. Suddenly he thinks he's a real dog.
Shetland ponies and squirrels, Malibu had it all.
— So what do you want to talk to me about that you couldn't discuss over the phone?
— Well, I suppose you've heard about my sister.
— No, why, she back in rehab?
— She's dead.
A belt wrapped tight around my chest.
— She OD'd?
— Yes, three weeks ago yesterday. I'm sorry Bobby, I was sure you must have heard.
She was right, I should have. When someone OD'd in AA, word traveled fast. Junkies and alcoholics find nothing more compelling than news of an overdose. Whether it was Clem who'd been clean twenty years before he relapsed and was found with his face in his plate at the kitchen table, or sweet little Danny, who died huffing a can of aerosol in a Starbucks bathroom in Reseda, these little fables were our bible stories, as exciting and gut-wrenching as only death can be.
— Angie, I'm so sorry. I don't even know what to fucking say.
— Had you seen her around much?
— No, but that doesn't mean anything, 'cause I haven't been around much. And the meetings I do go to are mostly men's stags.
— I guess it doesn't matter now anyway.
— I'm so sorry.
— Why? She was a girl with a death wish and now she's gotten what she wanted.
She said it almost bored, like it was her official statement on the matter; nothing like a nice sound bite to make sense of your grief.
— Do you want to know the details?
— No. I mean sure ... If you want to tell me.
— I actually found out from her counselor at Friendly House. She had called a few days before and asked me if I had heard from her, and I told her I hadn't because I'd been advised not to have any contact with her by my Al-Anon sponsor. I don't know what I was thinking letting some miserable, lonely woman dictate how I deal

with my own sister.

— Well, that's 12-step programs—you're supposed direction.

— Oh, please, for fuck's sake. Now I have a bigger resentment against her than I had against Carla.

She seemed more angry than torn up, but everyone has their own style when it comes to grief.

— The whole thing can be tricky.

— If tricky means bullshit, then yes, it's tricky. Anyway, she was found naked in the bathtub at some place called the Snooty Fox.

— Oh Jesus, really?

— Yes, why, is that bad?

Yeah, it was bad. "She's going to end up dead in a bathtub at the Snooty Fox" was the kind of thing you said about a certain type of junkie girl when you ran into her all smacked back, especially if she was unwashed and in the company of some shady-looking dude. But Carla wasn't that type at all. She was more the type to go out in a two-thousand-dollar-a-night room at the Chateau Marmont with Gary Oldman making the 911 call. The first time I saw her was at an AA meeting in Hollywood. She walked in, and every head in the room turned, even the women, especially the women. There was a vibration coming off her, the kind that comes off a great painting.

— What was she doing down at the Snooty Fox?

— Drugs, I imagine. Why, what kind of place is it?

— It's the Snooty Fox. You know, it's like hard-core, sordid South Central shit. Rooms by the hour to fuck and use in.

— So, what you're saying is it's not a wholesome place.

— No, there is no wholesomeness involved. It's got a certain style, but it's ... It's like the Waldorf Astoria for junkies and hookers. Was she turning tricks?

— Not that I know of, but I can't say it's impossible.

— Was she broke?

— She was never broke.

— Guess it helps to be beautiful.

— Didn't help her.

— Yeah, well, drug addiction is a motherfucker.

— They say it always wins in the end.

— Really, who says that?

— People who know.

— Oh yeah, what do they know?

— This is not a great time to be sassy with me, sweetie, though I usually like when you are.

— Sorry, don't let me interrupt.

I look up and some big red-haired dude is headed from the bedroom toward the kitchen. Oh, and he's naked ... Naked, uncircumcised and acting really casual with a really big dick.

4.

— I thought you were going to make me a juice, luv?

That was naked dude calling from the kitchen. I give Angie a little tsk tsk look.

— My, my, offering to make juices for everybody.

But she didn't feel like playing along, and instead sent her voice and attention toward the kitchen.

— I haven't gotten around to it.

— Ahhh. Too busy talking to the Yank.

He had a Scottish accent. Strong enough to be irresistible, weak enough to be understandable.

— There might be some from yesterday in the blue pitcher, sweetie, or give me a moment and I'll whip up a fresh batch.

Not only was she making juice for every naked Scotsman who blew through, she had given my pet name away. I shifted my weight, trying to find a soft spot in one of the dark wood, high-backed dining chairs. They would have made great set dressing for a play about the Spanish Inquisition.

— I really do appreciate your jumping in the car and trekking up here.

— No problem. Who's the naked dude?

I tried to sound, casual, like his entrance into the scenario was the most natural thing in the world.

— Liam, he wants to know who the naked dude is.

— Why does he want to know?

The Scottish king had a smile in his voice.

— Why do you want to know, Bobby?

— 'Cause I'm a sweet and curious boy.

Calling out to Liam,

— Because he's a sweet and curious boy.

— Well poor fucking you, laddy, that's a hell of a way to go through life.

He had come out of the kitchen, smiling, and holding a large bottle of dark beer.

I raised my eyebrows at the bottle.

— Passed on the juice, huh?

— Beer before noon and you'll sing a happy tune.

Now it was my turn for a fake laugh.

— I'd offer you a tug. But you can't drink, right, cause you're sober? Poor fucker, you shoulda shown some self-control and not gone shootin' a bunch of smack like a mad banshee.

She must have been a little guilty about telling him I had been a junkie, because she looked over to see my reaction.

— Don't get me wrong, I'm glad you found your way to the wagon. That's why Ange's got you up here, eh?

I didn't really know what he was talking about, but I smiled like I did. He tilted back the bottle, swallowed hard and wiped his beer mouth with the back of his big hand. He was a fucking pirate, and freckled from head to toe.

— I'm not making you uncomfortable, am I?

— The beer or the birthday suit?

— Take your pick.

Liam took another swig and spread his thighs a little further apart. He was marking his territory like it was a David Attenborough documentary.

— You take that thing with you everywhere?

He smiled, and winked, his orange eyelash crunching down on his cheek.

— When you own a Ferrari, you don't leave it parked in the garage.

I hate it when I start to like someone I've made up my mind not to.

— You keep glancing at it, Robert. Little gay, are we?

— He's not gay.

She said it with a snort, then casually threw in,

— Liam is Carla's brother.

— Oh.

I said it as if that clarified something, but it didn't, and my brain started working double-time.

— So, you two are brother and sister?

— No, we're not related. Carla and I had the same mother, and she and Liam had the same dad.

— So, we aren't sibs. We're close as sibs, but we're not sibs. Understand?

I was starting to. Liam turned over the bottle and drained it, his large Adam's apple bobbing in his red sleeve of a neck. He brought the empty down hard on the table.

— I believe my work here is done.

He stood and extended his hand toward me.

— Pleasure to meet you, Robert, hope it all works out with Ange, and this business with "Carl."

He extended his hand and I stood and shook. I'd never shaken hands with a naked man before and wasn't quite sure how I felt about it. He turned and strode toward the bedroom like a big roan horse headed back to the paddock, his pale white ass the only freckle-free zone on his body.

When I sat back down Angie was looking at her phone. She put her finger in the air to let me know she needed a moment, that I hadn't been forgotten. She punched at the screen with a pampered finger, then looked up at me as if everything was just peachy.

— Your almost-not-quite brother enjoys lounging before strangers in the nude.

Her text pause had given me a moment to write that one in my head.

— He's always been a bit of an oddity. Needs to show everyone his big prick. It's painfully infantile, but you know men. Hope he didn't put you off.

— No, he put me right where I need to be.

I had no idea what that meant, and neither did she, but she still gave a savage little half-smile that made her top lip disappear.

— So you guys sleep in the same bed?

— We have, why? Lots of brothers and sister sleep in the same bed.

— Yeah, when they're four and six. And I thought you weren't brother and sister.

— We're not.

— Then what are you?

— I don't know what we are.

— But you sleep in the same bed?

— You want to know if we fuck?

— Well, I'm not sure I *want* to know, but tell me anyway.

— Well, we haven't slept together recently, but yes, we have had sex. I took his virginity when he was seventeen.

— That's very British of you.

— I knew you'd say something like that.

She scratched the nape of her elegant neck, then put her hands flat on the table.

— Have you ever seen anyone overdose, Bobby?

I knew the answer, but let the question take a slow lap in my bloodstream.

— Yeah, why?

— Have you ever seen anyone die?

— No. I've seen a lot of people go out, but I've never had anyone die on me. I've had to bring a few back though. When people die, they usually die alone.

— But you never just left, just left them there.

— No, that's not my style.

It was true. It wasn't my style. My style was to go into heavy action. "Heavy action" consisted of shaking, slapping, and in the case of one crazy, little Russian speedballer named Igor, blowing into his breathless body like I was blowing up a raft.

— Well, I think there was someone with Carla down at that hotel, and I think he just left her there. And robbed her as well.

— What makes you think that?

— Her bag was gone when the police got there.

— How do you know she had it with her?

— My God, Bobby, she wasn't homeless. Of course she had her bag with her. Maybe he even gave her an extra strong dose, so he *could* rob her.

— So, now you think it was murder?

— I'm not sure what I think.

— Was it a guy she knew?

— Yes.

— Her dude?

— You mean pimp?

— No, I mean boyfriend. Was it her boyfriend, a dealer, a running partner?

— I don't know if they were involved romantically, I just know they were using drugs together. At least that's what the woman at Friendly House told me, that Carla had been spending time with this boy, and that they had been using drugs together and that she thinks he was there when it happened.

— She's not sure?

She shook her head.

— Why doesn't she ask him?

— No one can find him.

— And what, you want to talk to him?

— I'd like to know what happened.

— I can tell you what happened. She overdosed. If this guy was there, he either panicked and left her like a scumbag, or he tried to save her, and then left her like a scumbag. Or maybe he just got scared. It's scary when people overdose. And you don't know, he might have had cases, or was on parole or something. I mean we're talking about real junkies here. Junkies don't wait for the police. Unless it's like the love of your life. People OD'ing is an occupational hazard.

— Sounds like a charming way to live.

— It may not be charming, but it's real. All I'm saying is, I don't think knowing what happened is going to make it any less painful and it might make it more.

— I don't care, I want to know the truth.

— I just told you the truth. You mean you want to know the details.

Suddenly her blue green eyes were slate gray, and her shame halo had turned to little horns.

— Okay, I'm going to be honest with you, Bobby. I don't care whether he stayed or left. I care about the bag!

— Why, what's in the bag?

— A ring, my mother's engagement ring. It's not terribly valuable, but it has a great deal of personal meaning. Carla never wore it and kept it in a little hidden flap in her wallet. If you didn't know it was there, you'd never find it.

— That means he's got to still have the wallet.

— I know. I had it handmade for her in Florence. It was one of the few trips we went on where we got along I'd love to get that back as well. I know this all must sound sentimental—

— No, I get it … It's just a lot can happen in three weeks, and you don't even know for sure he was there.

— Someone had to take her bag.

— That could have been anyone. It could have been the dude who works at the front desk. He's probably got a whole side business selling the shit people leave in rooms.

I don't know why I was raising so many questions. Maybe I was just feeling a little protective of the guy. I didn't know what he did or didn't do, but when in doubt, I always side with the junkie.

— The only way to sort any of this out is to find him.

— So find him.

— I want you to find him. I told you on the phone I'd pay you.

— You're going to pay me to find some junkie?

— Yes.

— I'm a writer, not a bloodhound.

— I know you're a writer, but an out of work one at the moment or am I wrong?

I hadn't had a paying gig in three years and a well paying one in five. The only thing between me and a tent on the street were residual checks and pity.

— Not exactly out of work, but I haven't started getting paid yet for the work I am doing.

— Well I'm offering to pay you.

— How much?

— So, you're going to do it?

— I didn't say I'm doing anything, I just asked how much?

— I don't know, whatever you think is fair.

— I don't know what's fair.

— Well, think about it.

I tried to come up with a number, but the monetary value of my time had become a pretty abstract subject.

— What do you think is fair?

— I have no idea. Something more than driving an Uber but less than running an oil company.

— How's five hundred dollars now, another fifteen hundred when I find him, and then three grand if you get the ring back. That's five thousand total.

— Sounds perfect.

Fuck I should have asked for more.

— But get the wallet as well, it's a little piece of perfection.

— Well, if I'm going to get the ring, I'm sure I'll get the wallet.

— Good. I'll go fetch my checkbook.

She got up, walked toward wherever her purse was, and called out.

— Carla's counselor says you know him.

— Oh yeah, what's his name?

— His name is Kyle Strange.

Carla's counselor was right.

5.

It isn't even noon and the line at the fish-and-chips place has already spilled onto the PCH, but I am feeling neither patient nor hungry. What I am feeling is a dull ache in my chest as I think about what happened to Carla, and whether Kyle Strange's hands aren't the only ones that might have a little dirt on them.

It was a couple of years ago, near the end of my thing with Angie. I was sitting at the Insomnia Café trying to get the words to behave when I get a long text from a number I don't know: "Hi Bobby, It's Carla. I got your number from Blake, hope that's okay :)." What you said this morning at the meeting really made me laugh, about how god wants us to walk to him, but the devil sends a limo. It's true. Wondering if maybe you have time to meet this afternoon for a cup of something, hopefully somewhere on the east side ... And it's probably best for both of us if you don't tell my sister."

I felt like I had swallowed a butterfly collection. What could Carla Batson possibly want with me? I'd seen her in meetings and never gotten more than a wary nod and now here she was quoting my share and requesting an afternoon rendezvous. A rendezvous to be kept on the down low.

We made a plan to meet at the Café Vita in Los Feliz. When she was ten minutes late I was unfazed as I was expecting it, but when it went to twenty I got a little cranky. I mean, here I am just minding my own business, making believe I have a life when she drops her little mystery bomb in the middle of my day. And now that she's got me drunk with anticipation, she blows me off just to teach me a lesson. And you know what, I deserved it. You don't meet the woman you're seeing's sister on the side for "coffee," especially after she makes it a point to tell you it's on the side ... Especially that sister. I looked out the window in mid-self-castigation and whap, there she was, lost in a cigarette and lanking across Sunset like an off-duty Katharine Hepburn.

She walked in, spotted me in the back, and ambled over. She was wearing a red Montreal Canadiens hockey sweater, and wearing it well. I stood to shake hands, but she came to my side for a hello hug. I expected something English and airy, but she pressed into me like we were finally meeting after a long correspondence. When she pulled away there were tears in her eyes.

— Well now you know I'm fucking crazy so at least we've got that out of the way.

I want to describe her in detail, do justice to who she was and try to capture the singular hum that I felt coming off her cells but I'm not sure that's doable with words. It was beyond her physical beauty. It was what was going on inside her, the weight of her inner life. It pulled in everything that wasn't bolted down. I tried to be all chill, but I couldn't not look at her ... She carelessly demanded it. Just the way she brought the coffee cup to her mouth with both hands like it was her first sip of water after a trip across the desert or how she caught my eye little waif style, as she licked the chocolate icing from the foil of her five-dollar ring ding. And yes, the color of her mouth and that little space between her teeth and the way she'd been marked by all she'd been through.

She was better than gorgeous. She was battered to an imperfection that perfection can't touch. She just made sense to me and so did how she'd gone about it. Life had presented us with its wounds and wonders and we had both come up with the same solution: The suede-soft self-hatred of junk.

— I took a ninety-day chip yesterday.

— Good for you, that's no joke. Those first ninety are brutal.

She looked at me and smiled.

— It isn't real. I've been using the whole time ...

An involuntary moan came out of me. Lying about your sobriety time felt even worse than using.

— Does anybody know?

She shook her head.

— Yuck.

She sniffed a laugh through the doom.

— What are you going to do?

— I don't know ... I'm not going back to another rehab, I can't. I just need to get away somewhere and kick.

I nodded my head even though what she said made no sense.

— I found an Airbnb in Murrieta Hot Springs, was thinking to go there and take Suboxone and Klonopin for a few days, then just soak in the baths and tough it out.

— You really think you can do that? I'm not saying you can't, but junkies aren't great at "toughing things out." At least I wasn't.

— No, I can do it. I just need someone to hold my meds and keep an eye on me.

— You mean like hire a sober companion?

— No, no more sober companions. To be honest I was hoping *you* might come with me.

6.

I walk into the Chase Bank on La Brea or, as I like to call it, the Chabad Lubavitch Savings and Loan. There are four people in line in front of me, three are Hasidic Jews, two of whom are Lubavitchers and wear the black Borsalino fedora particular to that community; I guess even God likes a nice Italian hat. The third Hasidim is right in front of me. He smells like garlic and old books and has Shirley Temple curls dangling like Talmudic earrings. His hat is more of a Quaker Oats pork pie and right up my alley. I consider grabbing it and running, but just admire it instead.

I step up to the window and my teller is wearing a sky-blue shirt that says "Chase" on it. I guess they want her to seem like a member of their bowling team, not the robot employee of a soul-crushing, financial Golgotha. Her name tag says "Zamine" and she is done up in a way that only an Armenian girl would even try to pull off. Her top lip alone has enough pink gloss on it to frost a cake and she isn't "wearing" rouge, she's been wounded by it. Every feature on her face is its own principality, from the swooping green eyes to the double bump nose to her innocent yet vicious mouth. I can't see her bottom half cause of the teller window, but the swell of her Yerevan chest makes the bowling shirt as glorious as Joseph's coat.

— What can I do for you?

— Just depositing a check.

She looks at me like she immediately understands everything there is to know about me, and couldn't care less.

— Stick your card in please, chip first.

I stick my card in the machine on the counter and the chip assesses my entire self-worth. I have forty-nine dollars in my corporate account, twenty-six dollars in my savings account, and seventy-three dollars in my checking account. I'm a man of the world.

I sign Angie's check and push it over.

Zamine looks at my mark, which is somewhere between a squiggle and a spasmodic reaction to shock treatment.

— That's your signature?

— Yeah, it's the only one I can do the same way twice.

She giggles a pink smile and for a second, I think I've actually won her over with my old soul-lost boy charms. She bites the laugh off hard, and gets back to business.
— When will the check clear?
— Midnight.
— How much can I get now?
— Let me look.
She is disgusted by my poverty, but that's only going to make her love me more in the end. She turns to check something, and I get my first look at her bottom half. It's a matching set with the top. I think about the way her neck might smell and whatever else my nose might wander into and get a little giddy. I'm usually the dirtiest boy in any given room, but with all these Hasidim around, I'm an underdog.
— One hundred forty-eight dollars. That is the total of your three accounts.
— Okay, just give me a hundred.
I put the dough in my pocket and head out. When you've been walking around with a ball of crumpled singles, five crisp twenties makes you feel like you own the world. I push through the door, and back into it. The wind is starting to falter but manages one more gust just for show. There's an old, goat-beard Hasid huddled at the ATM machine, digging through a leather pouch that holds his tallis, a hundred grand, or both, then I have to sidestep two Jewesses each with baby carriages, and dressed like they're going to a "League of Women Voters" luncheon, circa 1958. If these are my people, I have no idea who I am.
I make the parking lot and am about to get in my car when I hear, "Yo Zorn." I bring my head around, and a very straight-looking white dude is walking right at me, and I mean so straight that he's hip.
— Floyd Digbee. What are you doing over here, man? I didn't know they let you this far west.
— Just getting some funds before I hit this rental house. I thought that was you.
Floyd was a cat I knew from the program, a hotshot art director, and a bad junkie back in the day. Now he was more concerned with what private school to send his kids to than getting to the methadone clinic on time.
— What are you doing tonight?

It was quite possibly the worst question one could be asked.

— I'm busy, unless whatever you got is better than what I'm busy with.

I couldn't say that to everybody, but I could say it to Floyd.

— I'm filling in as secretary at the Alvarado meeting, and I don't have a speaker.

He looked at me figuring there was no way in hell I'd say yes.

— Well, I'm your man.

The answer surprised us both.

— Right on, dude. That's great. Those kids'll be lucky to hear you. You can tell 'em about the ants.

I smiled.

— We'll see. Might be a little close to dinnertime for the ants.

He laughed.

— That's a gnarly tale, dude.

— It is. It's nice to be on the other side of it.

— Tell me about it.

We shared a knowing smile. There's nothing better than being an ex-junkie. You get to have lived the life, but you don't have to live it no more.

7.

It's already dark, as I park behind the taco truck on Alvarado. They're just setting up, and the heavy-set forty-something Latina proprietor is laying out sliced cucumbers, and that milk-thin guacamole salsa that I want to like but never do. She wears flip-flops, swap-meet designer jeans, and barely lifts her feet when she walks. She's had a few bad breaks and even more bad boyfriends. She gives me a dignified nod. I catch it with my eyes and give her one back. Sometimes a moment on the street with a stranger is worth more than all the friends in the world.

I head up toward Sunset and the church where the meeting is, and it occurs to me that this meeting, this Monday night at 8:00 p.m. Sunset and Alvarado meeting is where I first met Kyle Strange. It was back in 2011, and I was finally off the last of my methadone and as close to in my right mind as I get. I was sitting next to the long table where the coffee is, snaggin' the occasional Trader Joe's Oreo, when I hear this dude start his share. And the minute he opens his mouth, he's got my attention.

He's talking about seeing his father for the first time in ten years, and how he has a week clean, but his dad really wants to get high, and gives him some money to go cop for them, and then when they get down, his father can't find a vein, so he has the kid shoot him up, and, of course, the father OD's and dies, only he doesn't really die; the kid is somehow able to bring him back. And I'm like holy fuck, all my father ever did was miss a few little league games. After the meeting I was out on the sidewalk smoking one of my three weekly cigarettes and wondering what it would be like to fuck a girl with a "Cramps" tattoo on her neck, when the "Chief," a good looking, half-queer Mexican hipster brings the kid over to me, and says, "Bobby, this is Kyle." Then he turns to Kyle, and says, "Bobby was a bad junkie. Bad like us, worse than us maybe." Then the Chief turns to me. "Why are writers always the worst junkies? Anyway, you two should talk," and the Chief walks away.

— That was a deep share, dude.

— Yeah, the whole thing was kinda fucked up.

— Dear old dad.

He didn't have a cent, so I took him to the Bright Spot Diner and

ordered us a couple of patty melts. And over fried onions and
gooey cheese, he told me that he had gotten out of jail last night and
had already fixed this morning, and that he thought he could be an
illustrator if he could just stop using long enough to find out. I took
to the kid immediately. I'm not even sure why. I guess I just liked
the flavor of his self–loathing, and after he ate the last of his fries,
I drove him home, and told him to call me the next day.

— Dude, even if you don't want to, even if you've already used,
even if every cell in your body is telling you nothing will ever work,
just call me. Get military about it. Make believe you're Private
Strange.

He scoffed with a little dope fiend gleam.

— Private Strange. I'm *Colonel* Strange.

The next day, to my complete shock, he called me. And he called
me the day after too, and the day after that, and the day after that
and he kept calling, and the point of all that is, what Angie had
heard was true. I did know Kyle Strange, and not only did I know
him, I had been his AA sponsor. His sponsor, his pal, his older
brother, his private chef and part-time banker. I hadn't talked to
him or seen him in a good while, but I still loved the kid, and now,
somehow, I was getting paid to find him.

8.

What it was like, what happened, and what it's like now. That's the classic formula for a proper 12-step share. I'm sitting at the head of a big square of folding cafeteria tables, in the meeting room of a drab 1940s church. There's about twenty-five people around the tables, and another forty to fifty in folding chairs against the walls. That makes roughly seventy-five bad childhoods and at least four hundred tattoos. I have no idea what I'm going to say for fifteen minutes but talking about myself has never been a problem. It doesn't really matter anyway, I'm not going to get anyone sober, keep anyone sober, or change anyone's life.

The best thing to do is just stick with the facts, which are: I had dabbled with heroin as a teenager, and somehow escaped addiction while a lot of my friends didn't, and then after a few years being an actor in Los Angeles it all caught up with me. It got real dark, real quick, and the whole thing probably would have run its course, except a funny thing happened along the way: I fell into a successful screenwriting career. I was making money, eating lunch on the lot and shooting up three times a day in the old Disney Animation building men's room. I knew I had to get clean, but when they're paying you fifty grand a week to write fart jokes, you get clean later. Two years became five became ten became twenty, and with the screenwriting career now long gone, I was finally ready for the "what happened."

— So, one day in 2007, I wake up with a fever, and like any delusional junkie, I just figure I need to get "well," but the dope's not making me feel better, the fever's getting worse, and now I'm puking. I can't hold anything down. What do I do? Shoot more dope, and now my fever is over 105 which is extremely high for a grown-up. I haven't held down food for five days, and I'm so weak I can barely breathe, but my ex somehow gets me in the car and takes me to the emergency room. They do a bunch of tests and then this lady doctor comes in and says to me, "Bobby, you are a very, very, very, very, very sick man. You have endocarditis and your heart valve is coming apart and if you don't have open heart surgery you're going to die." I just started to cry. Not because I was scared or even because I thought I was going to die. I started to cry because I thought for all these years that I had been getting away with something, that I was a special case, and that I could pull off the un-pullable and cheat God and live a wild, rule-less life with no accountability to anything, and when she said that to me, I realized I couldn't, and that I had spent the last twenty years living a complete and total lie. A lie that now might kill me. They did a surgery called the Ross procedure where they took my pulmonary valve and put it on my aortic valve and put some dead guy's frozen valve where my pulmonary goes, and it worked. But they couldn't medicate me, 'cause my opiate tolerance was so high. They sawed my chest in half and let me scream for five days. And just as they're about to roll me out of intensive care, I start to bleed internally. They can't stop it. I end up bleeding out my ass for thirty-six hours, they don't know what to do; they can't stop it. Then a new doctor comes in, manages to clamp the wound and save my life. I had all these tubes in me and if I laid down I got nauseous, so I sat up in a hospital chair for thirty-five days and all I could think was, this is the worst thing that will ever happen to me, but in the end, it turned out to be the best thing, because there was no other way I would have ever stopped. That's what it took.

The timer went off. I didn't even get to what it's like now.

#

After the meeting I'm out on the sidewalk smoking a cigarette, when I notice Claude, a cat I know, tucked in the church doorway, hands in his pockets, filter-less Camel dangling. He's with some girl and they're posed just as nonchalant as any two little troublemakers can be. I catch his eye, and he gives me a nod on the inhale. I hadn't spotted him in the meeting, but he was someone I wanted to see.

— What's going on, kid?

— Gnarly sermon, brother. My virgin ears weren't ready for that much detail.

He nodded his eyes toward the girl, a mid-twenties pouty mouth with dark curls spilling out of a purple crochet cap.

— This is Isabella.

I kept it corny and gave her a salute. She looked past me and said:

— My father had a Ross procedure.

— Hey bro, let me get a word with you about something.

I turn to Isabella.

— Mind?

I pull Claude over to the corner and put his back against Alvarado.

— You seen Kyle?

— Fuck no, no one has.

— Have you talked to him?

He shook his head.

— He sent me a text last week, just to let me know he was alive.

— Why, is there a reason he shouldn't be?

— No. It's just, you know ... People are talking a lot of shit.

— No, I don't know.

— Well, you must know something, or you wouldn't be asking me about him. You guys don't talk anymore.

— That's not true.

— Yes, it is.

— Just because I haven't talked to him doesn't mean I don't care about him.

He gave me a dubious look. It hadn't even been twelve hours and I could already tell getting paid to find people was a creepy thing to do.

— You know anything about what happened?

— Just what I heard.

— What'd you hear?

— That shit happened.

— Come on dude, it's me, just tell me what you know.

— I don't *know* anything ...

He took a pull on his cigarette like only a junkie can.

— Someone heard that they were fucking, and he had a belt around her neck, and that it might have been auto-asphyxiation.

— That sounds like wishful thinking ... Besides auto-asphyxiation is when you do it to yourself, hence the "auto" part.

— Oh, right, like *Kill Bill*.

He meant David Carradine, not the actual movie.

— What was really going on with them, do you know?

— What do you mean?

— I mean was he copping for her, using with her, what was going on?

— They were together.

— Together like a couple?

— Yeah, like full-on.

It was such an absurd notion I have trouble taking it in.

— Kyle and Carla Batson?

— Yeah. The couple of times I hung with them, she was all goo-goo eyed for him.

— Are you serious or kidding?

— It was crazy. She was way into the dude, like way, way into him.

A wave of jealousy went through me, or maybe it was disbelief.

— When was the last time you hung with them?

He thought about it. But then I saw something click, and he pushed back.

— Why you so interested?

I didn't want to tell him I was getting paid to track him down like a bounty hunter, so I just let the question die on the sidewalk. Then *I* pushed back.

— How long you got?

He looked at me like it was an unfair question.

— Six weeks. I haven't used in six weeks.

— You on Suboxone?

He gave me the shame nod.

— Were you getting high with Kyle?

— Maybe, once or twice. The last time I saw him he just got me some Xanax.

— From who?

— Some old black dude in the hood.

— Down by the Coliseum?

— I don't remember.

— Was the guy named Robert Lee?

He didn't have to answer that one. The "yes" was in his eyes.

9.

DreamWorks is out in Burbank and getting there always tweaks me because you have to remember whether it's east or west on the 134 and even after thirty-three years here, the 134 is still a mystery to me. As I drive, I think about what I always think about when I drive to a studio, which is the past, how I fucked it all up, and in this specific case, how I fucked it all up with DreamWorks.

It was '96, and we had just finished rewriting Doctor Seuss's *Oh, The Places You'll Go!* Our script was a wild rhyming riff about identity, self-doubt, and all the rest of that good shit. It was green-lighted immediately and we were stoked. But then Seuss's widow read it, and with a wave of her liver-spotted hand, *Oh, The Places You'll Go!* was going nowhere. But the script was still strong and a month later it caught Jeffrey Katzenberg's attention. He, Spielberg, and Geffen had just set up their own studio, and it was big news. One of the first projects on their slate was an animated adaptation of an eight-page book about a farting green ogre.

Our first meeting with Katzenberg was like going to see the President. We were taken by one of his three secretaries through two sets of doors and into his private chambers. He was sitting behind his large black desk and waved us forward with a smile to let us know it was safe, even though everything seemed designed to let you know it wasn't.

He began with a quick monologue about how excited he was about the project, then stood and came out from behind the desk. He looked as if his head had been grafted onto the body of an eight-year-old boy. He sat down in an armchair and got right to it. Our script needed to have a "template," a non-animated movie that the whole thing should be based on, and the more iconic the better.

For the next two months we tried to come up with a "template," but he didn't like any of them, and neither did we. Then, one afternoon, I'm in the book, smiling at this donkey who gives the ogre a ride through the forest and it hits me. It's not an ogre movie, it's a buddy movie. A buddy movie about two disenfranchised oddballs. The ogre is Joe Buck, and the Donkey is Ratso Rizzo. My template is *Midnight Cowboy!* I'm ready for Katzenberg to tell me I'm nuts, but he loves it. We write for five months. They don't like a word and fire us ... But they keep the donkey.

#

I must have gone the right way on the 134 'cause I'm sitting in the reception area and feeling lost. That's what these places are designed for, to take you out of yourself. They make it real clear that they have something you want, and they'll decide if you get it. The trick is to remember that you have something they want, and they'd be lucky to have it. It's a trick I've never learned. Andrew and Nick are already there when I walk in. A midwestern blonde with no sharp edges emerges out of thin air. They're ready for us.

10.

— I love that poster, that's Czech, right? Ray collects Czech movie posters. He just got one for *War Games* that's this big black finger pushing down on a tiny little globe, it's all against a yellow background. It's really graphic, really cool.

That's Andrew Wood. He had a macchiato with two extra shots at the Starbucks on the lot, but it might as well have been an eight ball of coke.

— I think Ray's posters are Polish.

That was Nick, keeping it real.

— Czech, Polish, what's the difference?

— Well, the Czechs have a new wave, and the Poles have concentration camps.

Two minutes in and I've already thrown out a Holocaust reference. I mean business.

— It's actually Russian.

That's Dennis Destitrino. He's wearing a tight, black blazer and red Adidas with three-hundred-dollar jeans. Clearly, he's read the manual. The poster being discussed is for Andrei Rublev, a Tarkovsky masterpiece that can either change your life or put you in a coma depending on what time of day you watch it. Guys who make dumb cartoons for a living always need to show you how smart they are.

— Really, Russian?

That's Wood.

— I would have known if you had said it with an accent. I spent the weekend with two Russian girls down in the Mexican wine country, outside Ensenada. Ever been?

No one had.

— The wine's for shit, but it was good enough for these two. I was watching them go at it all weekend. They were really affectionate with each other. I tried to get in there, but they weren't having it, I was relegated to concierge duties, but it was solid viewing.

The current climate wasn't the best for this sort of public discourse and Destitrino tightened a little, but since there were no women in the room he gave Wood a pass. I don't think it mattered to the kid sitting next to him, a little up-and-comer named Evan who looked like he had just rolled out of a USC frat party. That's how they liked to do it, one guy with taste who looked like he stepped off a yacht, and one pudgy goofball who was as dumb as the nine-year-olds the movies were meant for. That goofball was the one who always made it big.

Destitrino turns to me and smiles a smile I've never had in my repertoire.

— So, what have you been up to?

I contemplated the question.

— Well, last year I won the Oscar for best screenplay and I have the number-one show on cable, that's why I'm here begging you to take me seriously.

Of course, I didn't say that, but when you've got nothing going on, and everything you're known for happened twenty years ago, that question has no good answer.

— Nothing particularly interesting.

Self-effacement is usually a good way to go, but not today. The line lays there like a blind cat that tried to cross the 405. But Wood didn't let it lay there long.

— So, how much do you guys know about this?

— Just what you told us, just the world.

— Well, we think this is timeless, usually we do things that are all about the zeitgeist, but this is bigger than the zeitgeist, the story is timeless, and the IP is completely untapped. I don't know why no one's thought of it, but they haven't, and I've checked with ten lawyers and they all say it's fair game and unprotected.

Wood had now contorted himself into a sloppy, manic pretzel and was rocking slowly, as he clutched at the shoe he had crossed in his lap.

— When I came up with it, I couldn't believe no one had been there already. I didn't tell anyone for days. I hid in my office, scared it was too good to be true.

— Well, you're not the only person to think of it. We've been playing in that sandbox for awhile, but we've never been able to crack it, so we're very interested to see if you have.

Little Evan seconded Destrino's interest with nodding eyes.

— Well, we think we have, or we think Bobby has.

And then like always happens when you're the designated driver/storyteller/screenwriter, all the attention finally turns to you, and you're on.

Pitching movies is black magic. It's part preparation, part charisma, and part con. Some cats are famous for being so charming in the room they could sell singing lessons to a deaf-mute, but I wasn't one of them. I had to fully believe in what I was saying, and if any part of it struck me as false I was sunk. In real life I could lie my ass off, but when it came to the world of make-believe I was honest as a boy scout.

I get out my pages. I got 'em in a Pee-Chee folder, like it's my seventh-grade book report.

— Nice Pee-Chee, you're taking me back.

That's Destitrino, he's back in my corner. I open the folder and take out the pages like I'm Itzhak Perlman pulling out his Stradivarius. I grab a silent breath, fight off a moment of shattering self-doubt, and get to the task at hand.

— Eleanor Rigby, Big Poppa, Black Magic Woman, Jumpin' Jack Flash. Who are they, and what do they mean to us? We've been hearing their names and listening to their stories for a long time, and it makes me wonder if maybe these songs, these undeniable masterpieces that have changed and defined the last sixty years of musical history, serve not just as the soundtrack of our life, but also as our modern-day fairy tales. And maybe, just maybe, the well-known characters of those songs are the untapped and cinematically untold Rapunzels, Cinderellas and Pinocchios of the present day.

I look up. Destitrino is smiling and little Evan is almost out of his seat. They get it; they understand Wood's breakthrough idea. He had found a legal loophole in popular culture and realized that what was protected in the great songs of the last five decades was the performance, and the copyright of music and lyrics, but *not* the characters. You could make a movie with a guitar-slinging lead character named Johnny B Goode, and he could befriend A Boy Named Sue, and they could hang out with the American Girl, or any of the endless iconic figures that populated the rock and roll songbook. All you had to do was come up with a story to hold it all, and I had. I told it to them. It was the fastest twenty minutes of my life.

11.

I pull out of DreamWorks and back into the world. Burbank lays flat like a board game, but instead of Park Place and Boardwalk, it's Pollo Loco and Bed Bath & Beyond. Yesterday's wind's blown everything out and the sky is so sharp and clear you can cut your meat with it. The San Gabriels are big, raw and white-capped and you can just about touch the snow with your tongue.

I turn onto San Fernando and the phone rings. Good news travels fast in this town, real fast. But it's Angie.

— Hey, you, what's going on?

— Are you driving, sweetie?

— I am indeed.

— So am I. I'm headed into town, and there's no one on the PCH. It's downright weird.

— Maybe it's a holiday?

— I don't think so.

— No, it is, it's National Rich, Lucky, Undeserving White People Day. Everyone is advised to stay home and hand-wash their Mercedes.

— My God, sweetie, you really are hostile. Amusing but hostile.

— I should put that on my business card.

— You're not the business card type.

— Oh yeah, what type am I?

— You're not any type, that's why I like you.

— I thought you didn't like me.

— Of course I like you. I was considering loving you, but you wouldn't give me a chance.

— That's one way of seeing it.

— That's the only way of seeing it. What are you doing? I was thinking about you, and that perhaps we should have an assignation ... That's a little get together.

— I know what an assignation is.

Actually, I had no idea what an assignation was, but you can't let these British birds get the upper hand or all hell breaks loose.

— Where are you?

— Just driving back from Burbank.

— You poor dear, what did you do to deserve that?

That was worth a chuckle, so I spit one out.

— Pitched a movie to DreamWorks.

— Go well?

— I don't know yet, but it felt good in the room.

— Well, then I'm sure it was good. Are you busy this afternoon?

— Not really, why?

The sign for the 134 came into view. I was ready for it this time.

— My friend from the BBC still has that company suite over at the W she lets me use when she's in London. Can you come over?

I took a moment to consider the question.

— To meet you at the W in Westwood?

— Yes.

— For what?

— So, I can see you.

— See me about what?

— My god Bobby, such distrust so early in the day. Maybe I'd just like to see your face and have a cup of tea without bad news to share, or my brother traipsing about naked.

— You don't need to bring me to a hotel for that?

— It's actually very nice there as I think you remember.

— Yeah, I remember.

— Why, do you not want to see me?

— I always like seeing you. You were the one who stopped taking my calls.

— Yes and now I've reached out to you twice.

— Lucky me.

She gave me the most English chuckle yet.

— Can you be here in an hour?

I had enough sense to give it a full measure rest before I said yes.

#

I get off the 134 at Forest Lawn where the best and brightest of L.A.'s dead Jews are schmoozing on the hill, keeping an eye on the Warner Bros. lot. The first time I heard the word *Burbank* was 1968. I was sitting in front of a nineteen-inch black and white Sylvania on the North Shore of Long Island with the old man when Gary Owens came on the screen, and with his hand cupping his ear, said, "Live from beautiful, downtown Burbank, it's Rowan & Martin's Laugh-In." That was fifty years ago. Half the cast is probably up there on that hill.

The phone rings again, and this time it says "Unknown." I feel a quick surge of heat and adrenaline; "Unknown Artists" is my management company. As I said, good news travels fast in this town.

— Hey.

— Bobby, I have Hildy for you.

Hildy Farkas was my manager. A fierce wrecking ball of a woman, she gave extensive script notes and suffered no fools, except me. Our initial meeting was at the Four Seasons hotel where she told me that her name meant "wolf" in Hungarian and that she protected her cubs fiercely but my chances for a comeback were slim. I ate some rubbery crabmeat, signed the theoretical papers and didn't hear from her for three months. An ex-packaging agent at UTA, she had two vocal styles: DMV lady with a toothache and schmoozy matchmaker, which I was getting now.

— Don't tell me someone's finally learning how to pitch after all this time?

— They liked it?

— Oh my god! I needed my thesaurus to keep up with the adjectives. Dennis Destitrino is in LOVE with you. LOVE!

And that right there is Hollywood in a nutshell. It's never you did a nice job, presented a good story that they are possibly interested in developing and making, it was always right to MOMMY LOVES YOU! You are loved, you have worth, you are not the piece of shit you thought you were when that guy at HBO said your idea wasn't fleshed out enough. You are the magical and brilliant little boy who Dennis Destitrino wants to kiss on top of the head and throw gold coins at. And even though I knew better, and had known better for twenty years, I ate it with a big, fat spoon, then got down on my knees and licked the bowl.

— He dug it, huh?

— He didn't dig it. It was *love*. Whatever you did today, bottle it, because he wants to get you in with Katzenberg as soon as possible.

Sixty different chemicals broke the dam in my brain and poured out over the upholstery. Hildy was still talking, but I could barely hear her. I tried to swim to her voice, but the waves held me under ... Katzenberg, Katzenberg ... My entire fate would come down to a rematch with Katzenberg.

— I have to jump because my horror movie is falling apart and I might have to fly to Akron, but Robert, I'm very proud of you. Your luck is changing, I can feel it.

12.

I pull up in front of the W and hand my little toy of a car over to a Mexican kid way too good-looking for the job. I never valet, but I'm now a big Hollywood screenwriter with an impending assignation, so I splurge.

I walk up the hotel steps, and some Ivy League sister comes at me, iPhone clutched in her butter-brown hand. She shoots me a look so dismissive it would put doubt into the Dali Lama, but I just tip my hat.

I'm fifteen minutes early, the last thing I want to seem is eager, so I sit down in the lobby, which looks like it was designed by a showbiz lawyer on Quaaludes. I lean back in a low-slung faux suede armchair and take in the crowd. The women are thin and brittle, and not one has the hair color on her driver's license. The men seem happier but it's hard to tell about what.

My phone rings. Maybe Katzenberg heard it was Zorn's project, and told them to just draw up the papers, and get the boy paid. I fish my phone out. It's a number I don't recognize, and it's got a big, long prefix. It doesn't feel like a bill collector, so I take the plunge.

— Hello.

— Robert, it's Liam, Ange's brother.

He didn't have to tell me, the accent already had.

— Hey, what's going on, man?

— Just wanted to call and say no hard feelings about yesterday?

— Hard feelings about what?

— Just felt like I might have put you off your game a bit, whatever meager bit of game you've got ... That was a joke, Robert, for fuck's sake, have a laugh why don't you?

— You just didn't give me a chance, dude. I was ready to have a huge guffaw.

— That's better, I don't trust a man unless he gives me a little cheek.

— Well worry not, I'm a very cheeky monkey.

— Are you now?

He took a beat and I heard a short exhale come out of his nose.

— Have you got a minute, Robert?

— Sure, I might even have two.

— Good, it might take two.

— What might?

He didn't answer and took another pause.

— Have you talked to Ange today?

The question was slippery with something ... I just wasn't sure what.

— No, I haven't heard from her.

I'm not sure why I lied except it was none of his business, and I didn't know the guy except for an odd five minutes with him, his beer, and his genitals.

— You don't know Ange very well, do you, Robert?

— Are you asking me or telling me?

— I know she was quite fond of you, or so it seemed. Isn't that right?

About ten different responses went through my head, but I settled on:

— We were quite fond of each other.

— She ever tell you about being engaged to the rock star when she was sixteen?

— You mean the drummer from Black Sabbath she was thinking about marrying. What about him?

— She wasn't thinking about marrying him, she was doing it. Her da had to go over with a hunting rifle and put some buck shot in his Aston Martin. Did she tell you her mother was in the bat house?

— Yeah, she did.

— She tell you why?

— Look dude, I don't know what this is about, but I don't need to hear her entire FBI dossier, okay. I'm not interested.

— Well, you should be.

— Well, I'm not.

— Well, you should be.

— Well, I'm not. I just want to see if I can find who she's looking for and try to get this ring back.

— It's not a fucking ring, Robert, that's why I've called you. She could give a pure damn for rings, or anything having to do with her crazy family. She's still got her mum's ashes in a paper bag in the bottom of a cupboard drawer! All I'm trying to do is open your bloody eyes for you.

— Well, thanks man, but I don't need my eyes opened.

— You need money, don't you? You want to be paid for your time?

— She's paying me.

— Paying you? She's laughing at you, Robert! Five thousand on a million dollars. That's half of one percent.

— The ring's worth a million dollars?

— Will you shut up about the fucking ring? It's not a ring she's after, Robert. The ring you can shove up your ass and shit into the river!

I look over and a Persian mother and daughter are watching me like I'm an Iranian soap opera. I get up and head for open space.

— Look, dude, I don't know what you're talking about, okay? She asked me to do something for her, and she gave me some money to do it. The rest is none of my business.

— Yeah, well you better make it your business.

I have a strong urge to ask him where he got my number or just tell him to fuck off, but that AA shit kicked in about showing "restraint of pen and tongue".

— Look, bro, I'm just going to hang up now, okay? Thanks for the call, it brought a lot to my day.

— Okay Robert, just calm down, I'm not looking to upset you. I'm just trying to bring to your attention that you're being played like a drum by our dear, sweet Angela, and that if you want to be paid in a manner that is more sympathetic to the situation you now find yourself in, then you're going to need to talk to me.

— What situation?

— You sure you want to know? I thought it was none of your business?

I looked up; it seemed like the whole lobby was staring at me. I headed for the restrooms.

— Look man, I can't talk about this right now.

— Oh, are my two minutes up?

— It's just not a good time, dude.

— Well, when is a good time?

— I don't know.

— What do you know, Robert?

— Dude, don't fuck with me right now.

— If this was on the up and up, you think she'd have called *you*? You're a bloody out-of-work writer. If this smelled right she'd have hired a professional weeks ago and the ring, wallet, whatever would be safe in her warm hand, but it doesn't smell right, it smells sour as a Frenchman's ass.

For some reason Gérard Depardieu popped into my head.

— She's playing you, Robert. And maybe she knows what she's doing, because from what I can tell, you seem more than happy to be played. Now, when are you going to call me back?

— I don't know.

— When, Robert?

— Later. If I call you back.

— Oh, you're going call me back. You want the money. And it's not even the Jew in you, it's the desperation. Now, when are you going to call?

— I don't know. And is this a European number? I can't afford a fifty-dollar phone call.

I didn't love asking after the "Jew" talk.

— Yes, it's Glasgow, but you won't be charged if you call it.

— You sure?

— Call me, Robert.

— Okay. We'll see.

— Call me, Robert.

And he hangs up.

I go into the men's room and straight into a stall. It has a white shuttered door like some kind of Bermuda resort. I look down at my phone, there's a text from Angie:

"Room 614 sweetie and there's a pot of tea brewing. Btw the terrace is right over the pool, something wonderfully South Beach tacky about it. See you in a bit — A."

13.

I get to Room 614, close my eyes, and try to pull my shit together. I already had mixed feelings about being at Angie's beck and call before Liam intervened to tell me she was full of shit, but now I really don't know what to think. I guess I could just handle myself like some kind of adult, actually observe her behavior and make my own assessment about whether she's lying or not, but if I still knew how to trust my instincts, I'd have a series on Netflix and not be running around chasing junkies. I take a breath and knock, nothing cute, just a solid two in rhythm.

She answers the door naked in a pair of heels.

— Are you kidding me?

— You don't approve?

— I didn't say that. I … I wasn't expecting it.

— I bought this pair of Laboutins in Paris and have never found the opportunity to wear them.

She strode by me into the middle of the room and did a full turn.

— How do I look, laughable or fuckable?

It was a good question, so I gave her the once-over. She looked good. Her appendix scar was right where I left it and pointed toward home like a neon arrow to a roadside diner.

— Are you going to kiss me?

I smiled, and stepped toward her, but instead of a kiss, I rested my hand on her throat.

— What are you going to do to me?

— Don't worry, it'll be in your best interest.

She chuckled nervously, her tiny Adam's apple dancing in my hand.

— Put your mouth on mine.

She said it in a breathy whisper, and we stood there a nice long moment, her blue eyes versus my brown ones.

— Come now, Bobby, are you here to stare or are you here to fuck?

I went to kiss her like she asked but something got a hold of me and I slapped her quick instead. She gasped like it made no sense and made all the sense in the world. The smile was gone. Her eyes got bluer and her lips got full. I took hold of her and burned a soft kiss into her just slapped mouth. She let out a purr that was the most female thing I've ever heard in my life. And suddenly I was free. If she was lying to me, then I'd fuck her like a liar, if she wasn't, then I'd fuck her like I'd always wanted to, but never had. It didn't matter. They were the same thing. It was all the same thing, all of it.

#

I'm out on the balcony in my boxers, looking down at the pool. A pair of young women from some brown clan are swimming in white bikinis, and if they have a care in the world they're hiding it well. As for me, I got a lot of cares, one of which is whether the woman in the bathroom is lying to me about why she wants me to track down Kyle Strange. At least she bought me postcoital room-service eggs, so that's another forty-spot on top of the five hundred I've already seen.

I'm embarrassed to admit my mind works like that, but it does. I was even thinking of cancelling the room service order and asking for the cash instead, but that would have been pushing it.

— My God, it's a scene out there, isn't it?

She's come onto the balcony in one of those white bathrobes they give you in these joints, sipping a cup of tea.

— Every time I come here those same two Persian men playing backgammon.

— Yeah, how often do you come here?

— Fairly often, more for work meetings than rendezvous.

I still didn't know if she was lying about the ring, but she was definitely lying about that.

— How were the eggs?

— Almost as runny as you.

She clucked a laugh and sat down.

— They really should put a pack of Dunhills in the drawer, next to the King James.

— Or Pall Malls.

I'm not sure she knew what Pall Malls were, but she smiled anyway.

— I have a very strong response to you, Bobby. It's primal. I felt it the moment we met. I was reading your energy signature.

— Oh yeah? Was it a good read or did you put it down halfway through?

— Don't joke, I'm serious. There's something in your touch. I've read that women cum most with men who are profoundly genetically dissimilar to them.

— Well, then you should fuck a baboon.

I was full of quips, but my mind was flying. Liam was right, I didn't know her that well, and the fact that we had just spent an intimate hour that had gone from savage to tender to room service didn't bring her any closer. In fact, the sex had had the opposite effect. I felt like I was looking at her through the wrong end of a telescope.

— Your crazy Scottish roommate called right before I came up here. He told me that you're lying to me, and that whatever it is you're after is worth a million dollars.

That's what I wanted to say but settled for:

— Every time I see you lately somebody's walking around naked.

— That does seem to be the case.

She crossed her ankles and threw her attention back down at the pool.

— My father played backgammon. He once lost fifty thousand quid in a weekend. You pushed it quite far today, Bobby.

— Did I? Sorry about that.

— No, you're not.

The blue eyes flashed, and her beach house brown leg pushed through white terrycloth.

— Not one little bit.

She leaned back and let the late afternoon light work for her. I'd rather be next to a beautiful woman who might be lying than a plain one sitting on a stack of Bibles.

— I've been thinking, sweetie ...

She looked up from the teacup in her terry cloth lap. The blue eyes turned up to ten.

— Now, I know this might sound a bit foolhardy, but I just can't seem get it out of my head.

— Oh yeah, what's that?

— Well, I have to wrap up some work odds and ends at the end of the month, but after that I have nothing holding me in Los Angeles. A dear acquaintance of mine has been invited to teach Italian literature for a semester at the University of Kyoto, he's a bit of a Japanophile, and can't resist. Anyway, he's offered me his farmhouse in Tuscany while he's away, and I'm thinking of taking him up on it. A few months in the Italian countryside with just Chagall sounds glorious, but now I've got it in my head that you should join and make it a cozy troika. After you've found Kyle, of course.

Money to find junkies, fancy hotel sex and a trip to Italy. She was full of generosity.

— You want me to come to Italy with you?

— I do. These aren't just idle musings, sweetie. I feel I can do a great deal of good for you, and I know doing it would do a great deal of good for me. All you need to bring is your laptop, and a satchel of clothes. Italy and I will take care of the rest.

14.

It's been there like a peach pit just below my solar plexus ever since I talked to Claude. I knew I wasn't going to call or even make a decision about when to go, I'd just be driving on Beverly or 6th when the car would magically turn and I'd be headed down Vermont, only this time when I crossed Washington I wouldn't turn onto the 10 and head for Alhambra and the pork fat safety of Sam Woo barbecue, no, I keep going, past Adams, and down to King Boulevard and that "Golden Bird" on the corner that sends the smell of week-old grease into the disenfranchised air. And I was right, the car did magically turn, only it wasn't 6th street, it was 3rd, and I didn't take Vermont, I took Normandie. I hit Jefferson and glanced at the strip mall with the Ted's Burger. There used to be two callback pay phones on the corner, where I'd page Kenny Butler. I'd say, "Hey man, what's up?" And he'd say "Same, same," in a narcotized drawl that got me even higher than the dope. Ten minutes later he'd swing by in a late '70s model Seville, either the maroon with the crooked grill or the pale yellow with a gray Bondo back door on the driver's side. He knew what a Pall Mall was, and his ash was as long as a Chinese king's pinky nail. I knew Kenny three years and now he's dead twenty-three, but he's still the coolest person I ever met by a mile. He was like a dad to me, a dad who sold strong white dope and drank Dr. Pepper in the can 'cause it was "colder than the bottle." I thought we'd be together forever, but the car accident changed all that. He nodded out on a stormy night and broadsided a semi at fifty miles an hour, going under the truck, and ripping the entire roof of the maroon Seville clear off. He had too much methadone in him to die right there, but a year or so later he was through. It was Kenny who introduced me to Robert Lee, Daffy, Big John, Honest John, Whiskey John, Crazy Jeannie, and Pete the Mailman. But it was Robert Lee who stuck.

I roll past the white box liquor store on Exposition, a windowless concrete bunker, the architectural style of which is post-modern food stamp. It sits on a crooked angle across from the generic Formica burger dive, where I used to order bad teriyaki from a Korean granny through bulletproof glass.

I hit Vernon, take a left and head east toward Vermont. This whole neighborhood gives me PTSD or maybe I already had it and these streets just bring it back. It's dark terrain, that's for sure, psychic and otherwise. I shouldn't even be down here without parental supervision and should have definitely run it by my sponsor, but that would have been too sane, too clean, too sober.

I head back up Vermont. I can feel the shadow world sending out its homing signal, pulling me forward like a magnet. I should probably say the Serenity Prayer, but maybe just thinking about doing it is good enough.

I stick in a Charles Mingus CD, hoping a little music will soothe the savage beast. Sounds like Howlin' Wolf and Beethoven sluggin' it out in the back room. Old Cholly never met a trombone he didn't like and soon the brassy heartbreak has cleared my muddled head, but it's not going to stay clear. It never does. I drive past a tire place, blaring its Aztec gold and red signage, and before I can say "llanta usadas", it's back. And when I say *it*, I mean my thinking. That Creature from the Black Lagoon. All of a sudden, I've got an e-ticket for Shadowland, and I know if I don't watch it, I'll be up to no good in a flash. Oops, I didn't watch it, and now I need to do something wrong. Need it like I need another breath. Need to hurt myself in some way that will feel great when I run to it, good when I'm doing it, and devastating when I'm done with it. That's the addict mission statement right there. A time-tested recipe of decision, action, and regret, and the regret is the high that lasts. The Mexican cartels might be all powerful, but they don't run the shame empire, and hungry junkies will get their fix from food, sex, love, gambling, exercise, fantasy, cigarettes, puking their lunch or picking their skin. It doesn't matter what they do, just that they do. The devil isn't in the details. He's in the decision, in the space between discomfort and action. That's where good and evil are played out. That's where God (whatever that is) and the devil (I know what that is) roll around on the ground like two actors in a bad B movie, each one trying to get the knife. It's where the rubber meets the road. In that vast spiritual ghetto between discomfort and what you decide to do about it. I've spent my life on those streets, and even when I somehow manage to make one good decision, there's always three bad ones, lying in wait.

Call somebody, Zorn, don't be reckless—you shouldn't be down here without a rope tied around your waist. I cross King going north, the L.A. Coliseum flanked to my right like a huge Roman cereal bowl. They built it in 1921 as monument to World War One soldiers, back when L.A. was orange groves and oil rigs, and the brothers couldn't live west of Central Avenue no matter how good they blew their horns. If I was the right kind of smart I'd just keep heading north on Vermont and not stop 'til I reach the valley, but I'm the wrong kind of smart, so I take the left on 39th, then two short blocks to Budlong, and there it is: a simple, two-story, Section 8 apartment building that's got the South Central genetic coding in every cell. I know I should just keep rolling, but I can't help myself and stop in the middle of the street to gawk, which is never a great move down here.

There's no car in Robert Lee's spot. The only cars I do recognize are two early '80s model Jaguar sedans, the pride and joy of the old Jamaican mechanic who uses the lot as his shop and whose name I forget, even though I talked to him every day for years. I look over to Robert Lee's bedroom window; the curtains are drawn. Old dope fiends don't like it light and bright. Then it hits me—that the Jamaican mechanic's name is Junior. That's when I hear—

— Yo, Bobby? That you?

I whip my head around to see Captain walking up from behind the car. It's not Robert Lee but I'll take it.

— What up, Captain?

— I thought that was you, what happened to the 4Runner?

— Oh man ... That shit's long gone.

Captain cackles. He's got the crazy laugh of a street alcoholic, even though he's a junkie and has been for thirty years.

— What you doin' in the street, why you ain't pull in?

— I didn't see Robert Lee's truck.

He was leaning over now, his face right in my window.

— You look good, man. That's what happen when you stop fuckin' with that shit.

He let out a sweet little burner of a laugh that came from his pack-a-day chest.

— Robert Lee out taking care of some business. He be back.

— That's cool, I was just in the neighborhood.

— Oh yeah, what you doin' down here. You ain't fucking up, is you?

— Not yet, least not that way.

This time he fired off a laugh like a shotgun. I pulled over to the curb, so he could get out of the street.

— You still fuckin' with them movies?

— Tryin'.

Captain had a hard, little bald brown nut of a head with some Afro scrub on the edges. His eyes were wild and bright and there was a nice little bipolar breeze blowin' at his back, though I had never seen its dark side. His ever-present smile was topped by a lush Billy Dee Williams mustache that was as black as the devil's heart. I forgot why they called him "Captain" but it was a common street name for the old cats in the neighborhood and there were probably ten different "Captains" between Western and Vermont alone.

— So, you goin' to them meetins? I need to get back to them meetins. Them meetins is good.

— Well, anytime you want to go just let me know.

— All right, cool man, I'll holler at you.

I smiled. Captain wasn't going to be going to any meetings, but it was a nice little bump of hope in his beat-down junkie day.

— Yo, Captain, you know Kyle, that kid Robert Lee was getting' them methadone tablets for, who I introduced him to?

Two minutes with Captain and I start talking like I'm a seventy-year-old brother from Watts.

— Yeah, I know him. Blonde hair Viking looking dude, but I ain't seen him since he ran into that trouble with that girl.

— You heard about that?

— Yeah, shame too, she was nice. Fine as a motherfucker.

— He brought her by here?

— Yeah, she be with him whenever he swing by. She was talking to Junior about buyin' one his old Jags, said her father had one just like it. You know I don't forget nothin' having to do with no cars, Bobby. She had some old motorcycle she was talking to me 'bout fixing up, old Triumph cafe racer. Even did some research on it, but when I go up to meet her to see the bike, she never show.

— Junkies.

That got another laugh out of him.

— You ain't lyin'. But it's a shame what come to her. Ain't nothing good ever happen at the Snooty.

I nodded my head. It was a nod I have never nodded at another white person in my life.

— You ain't seen him since that shit went down though, huh?

— No, but he come by and seen Robert Lee. Robert Lee said he was real shook.

— Robert Lee ain't say when he's coming back?

— No but should be soon. He out trying to stir some things up. You might check over with Mack. That old barber shop gone but he cuttin' hair out of a new spot down by 103rd and Avalon.

— Dicey part of town.

— Shiiitttt, you ain't lyin'.

— At least it's not Lynwood.

— Fuck Lynwood.

He snapped off another sharp laugh with a big nicotine echo.

— How's Mack doin'?

— He the same.

I flashed on the time I tried to get well in the bathroom of the barbershop on Western, and couldn't find a vein, and the owner of the shop banged on the door and hissed, "You better get your ass out of there boy." The memory made my toes cold. It was time to say goodbye to Captain and get the hell out of Dodge ... Either that or cop a bag and never leave.

— All right Captain, I'm gonna get. Tell Robert Lee I came by and I'll catch up with him.

— I tell him. Look here Bobby, you got ten dollars I can hold? I'm not sure when Robert Lee be back, and I might go over try to get me one of them things.

I reached into my pocket without pause and gave him the dough. Like I said, I always side with the junkie.

15.

The sign for Musso & Frank looms over Hollywood Boulevard like a neon speedball, the warm pink and cool green reminding you that the world was a better place when men wore hats. It was Liam's idea to meet there. I had called him as soon as I got home. I was planning on playing it cool for a day or two, but it was useless. He had a lit a fuse in my brain with that phone call and it was going to burn until I saw him.

I come in through the back, down two sets of three steps, through the swinging doors, and right into 1930. If the food was as good as the décor I'd eat here every night. I head up the narrow aisle of the dimly-lit room looking out for Liam, hoping I'll recognize him with his clothes on. There's meat grilling on an open hearth to my left, but all you can smell is old wood and air-conditioning. A wide Latino waiter with a head like a buffalo slips by in a scarlet wait coat with black lapels. He's got a tray of charred flesh and fried potatoes growing out his hand. If he knows your name you've done something right in your life. Not everything, but something. I see an arm go into the air and pull at me. Liam's rusty mane comes into focus, burning through the dimness like an orange lamp.

— Well, look at you Robert, right on time.

I slide in, put my back against the red leather, and look him in the eye like your father teaches you to when you're a boy. Though mine never did.

He took a pull on his drink, then looked down at the menu.

— Old Frank must have been a Scot 'cause they charge fookin' separate for salad dressing.

He swirled his ice and sucked down the last amber drops.

— What are you drinking?

— Scotch, Robert, always best to drink what you are.

He gives me a smile you give to a movie camera, not a man.

— A friend in the know says prime rib is the best way to go.

— Well, then you should order it.

— What about you?

— I'm not real hungry.

— Don't be a child, Robert, we're going to have a meal and a conversation. Now, may I order you a prime rib?

I tried to look at him like *he* was a movie camera, but the lighting wasn't as good on my side.

— Sure, go ahead.

— And what you would like as a side?

— I don't know ... They say you can see John Ford's reflection in the creamed spinach, so how about that?

— Wonderful, spinach for a growing boy.

He reached for a waiter and I reached for the bread.

— How do you know about this place?

— I've got a nose for places that serve red meat and scotch.

— We've all got our talents.

— Indeed. Seems at the moment no one's appreciating yours. Don't eat too much bread Robert, you'll ruin your appetite.

— Okay dad.

That got a smile out of him.

— So. What's worth a million dollars?

I said it casually like it was no big deal, but before he could answer the buffalo-headed waiter was ringside, holding his pad in a brown hand thick as the filet, and twice as tender.

— We'll have two center-cut prime ribs.

— How do you want it?

— Bloody as an unstaunched wench. And give us some cottage fries and a creamed spinach for Rabbi Robert here. And one more double Johnny Black and tell your man I grew up ten minutes from the distillery so act accordingly.

He flashes a grin that could charm the harpoon out of Ahab's hands.

— Bloody as an unstaunched wench. That's Shakespeare, Robert.

— I've heard of him.

— So, you've called me back. I'm quite surprised. I thought you were happy with two bits in your pocket and your head stuck in the sand.

— You're not going to answer about the million bucks.

— Oh, I'll answer, but first I need to know a few things.

— What do you need to know?

— I need to know if you think you can really find this fellow.

— That all depends.

— Depends on what?

— Depends on whether he's still out there doing his thing.

— And what do you think, is he?

— It's a good question. I'm not sure. I mean I don't know how freaked out he is or if some really sordid shit happened down there or what. There's also a chance he went somewhere to try and kick. That's what I'd do. When something really fucked up like that happens, you get to thinking that maybe this isn't such a good way to live your life, and you just want to go somewhere safe. Either that or you just say *fuck it* and start sharing needles with hookers.

He was finally looking at me like I knew something *he* didn't. I took a moment to enjoy it.

— Anyway, if he's in rehab I won't be able to get to him 'til he gets out. But if he's just out there on a tear we got a shot, because he's got to cop, and chances are he's going to cop from people he knows and most of the people he knows, I know.

— I see you've given it a bit of thought.

— There's nothing to think about. He's got a habit. He's either using, figuring out a way to use, or he's so flipped out he's off somewhere making believe he's going to kick. Those are his options. And then there's the .01 percent chance that he actually does kick.

I reached for my water glass to give my little dope fiend tutorial a chance to wash over him.

— Now, tell me about the million dollars.

He looked at me and past me at the same time.

— You ever hear mention of a man named Otto in your brief time with Ange?

I shook my head without moving it.

— She never mentioned the name Otto Schlein?

— No.

— You're sure?

— You think I wouldn't remember the name Otto Schlein? Who is he?

— He's an art dealer, a big one. He's who backed Ange in her gallery. And backed her other ways as well, and for a bit there Ange was under the impression that she was going to be Mrs. Schlein. But then she made the mistake of bringing Carla around, and let's just say that Carla got into Otto's blood in a way dear Ange never could. He became ... a tad obsessed.

I could relate.

— The right woman can do that to you.

— Indeed, she can. A year back or so Carla began tiring of Otto's act and took up with some big Hollywood director. This made Otto extremely pouty.

— What big director?

— It doesn't matter, Robert, he's not gonna hire you to write a movie.

— I was just curious.

— Otto wasn't happy with Carla's new arrangement and tried hard to win her back. There was a physical altercation at Mr. Chow, nothing too extreme, but enough for Carla to get a restraining order. Otto was so beside himself he gave Carla a series of original David Hockney pencil drawings as a token of apology.

— And that's what's worth a million dollars?

— You're a shamus of the highest order Robert ... *well* over a million. So, you see, it's not a ring that Angela's looking to retrieve, it's those drawings, and she wants them badly.

— Because she's mad at Otto for dumping her for Carla?

— Because she's mad at Otto, and because they're worth a million fookin' dollars.

— And why do you want them?

— Because Carla wouldn't approve if she knew they ended up with Ange.

He waved for the buffalo to check on his drink but missed him, then turned back and leveled me long and slow with his gold-flecked eyes. He reached for the inside pocket of his jacket and pulled out a white envelope. Then laid the envelope down on the table, keeping his hand on it.

— That's five thousand dollars. Ten times what Ange gave you. It's a key she wants, that's what's in Carla's wallet, the key to a storage space, and hopefully, and as important, the number of the storage space as well. You get that key from your friend Kyle and you and I shall open that lock together. If the drawings are in there I'll give you fifty thousand dollars, and on that you have my word.

He took his hand off the envelope.

— But if you pick up that envelope you work for me and not my fookin' sister.

16.

I got a call from Carla a few hours after we met at the Vita. She had gone ahead and rented the Airbnb in Murrieta and was "getting her affairs together" so she could leave. I had never really agreed to go with her, but I hadn't told her no and so she chose the version of reality more suited to her needs. I felt a rush of sickening excitement. She claimed to be asking me to go down to Murrieta for a few days and keep an eye on her, but what she was really asking was for me to lie to everyone I knew, including her sister, in order to save her life.

She said she'd come get me at nine, then we just needed to pick up the Suboxone before we got on the road. Something told me I should ask to take my car so I had some meager control over the situation, but as conflicted as I felt about going, I was even more scared she'd change her mind. I told her I'd text her my address, and as I was about to hang up she mentioned that she might "bring a little something for tonight and make a clean go of it tomorrow. But don't worry, I won't give you any even if you beg."

I don't know how it feels to commit a bank robbery or walk point in the jungles of Vietnam, but it can't be too different from how I felt when I hung up that phone. I knew I had no business running off with a using junkie, but it didn't matter. I just wanted to be near her. She had planted a seed in my belly, and in three short hours that seed had grown into a tree.

17.

I wake up with a head full of nonsense and a film of beef fat coating my tongue. It's not even six, and the light is scattered. It feels like I'm the last man on earth, but I know that's not true because I can hear the cars out the window. I walk over and pick my pants up off the floor. They got an envelope with five grand in them. That should take care of this morning's coffee. I might even treat myself to an eight-dollar slice of toast with a nice smear of artisan preserves. The culture may be going to hell in a handbasket but it's a great time for jam.

I'm back on Larchmont. I got my coffee, but I passed on the toast. I must be having a tough morning because one of the local yoga ladies is looking pretty good to me as she waits for class with her rolled-up mat. She's got a great nose and her mouth doesn't have that aching half-frown that is the signature of the devastated middle-aged female. You want to know what's going on emotionally with a woman in her fifties, don't look in her eyes, look between her nose and chin. I pull out my phone and start to make a list of things to do for the day.

1. Put five grand in bank.
2. Write a decent sentence.
3. Maybe take a swim or something.
4. Find Kyle Strange.

The yoga lady sits down at the table next to me. Her hair is Argentina brown and turns gold at the edges like she just ate the sun with a spoon.

I add "don't shit the bed" to my "to do" list when my phone rings in my hand like a joy buzzer. It's Suspicious Entertainment. When show business calls before 9 a.m., it's usually interesting.

— Hello.

— Zorn. It's Wood.

I was expecting the mellifluous tones of his assistant Colleen, but I got the madman himself.

— What are you doing at work so early?

— Reading scripts.

— Anything good?

— No, they're all shit, and big writers too.

— Well, I'm sure they'll all be green-lit immediately.

— Have you ever read Henry Miller?

— Is that a joke?

— No, why, you love him?

— Let's just say I'm a fan.

— A friend of mine wrote a script about him. About when he lived in Big Sur and people camped out on his lawn and thought it was a sex cult.

— Live action or animated?

He choked out a garbled laugh that sounded like part of a 911 call.

— Look at you, already funny at eight in the morning.

— Actually, I'm still funny from last night. What big writers?

— Huh?

— Which big writers wrote the bad scripts?

He whipped through a quick list, all with gentile first names, Jewish last names. If your name was Caleb Schwartzman it was a great time to be a screenwriter.

— How's the Henry Miller script?

— Needs a rewrite. You'd be perfect for it.

— Any money?

— Not yet.

— Than I really am ideal.

— Dude, we're going to sell this thing to DreamWorks, there's no question. I got some good ideas on ways to change the pitch. Come over and we'll talk about it.

I got a sinking feeling in my chest. If there was one thing I had learned in twenty-five years of writing it was that "talking about it" never led anywhere good.

#

Before I headed over to Suspicious, I stop at the bank to drop off the funds I had gotten from Liam. Zamine is stationed at her post, and I catch her eye from the line, as she waits on some tzitzit-wearing giant, his tiny yarmulke sitting on his bald head like a suede pasty on a huge, misshapen tit. He puts a nice slice of dough in an envelope and moves on. I step forward.

— You're back.

— I am.

— What can I do for you today?

Her eyebrows were like two dark forests. I smile at her.

— What?

— You have great eyebrows.

— Thank you, but I don't like compliments.

— How about deposits?

I pull out the five Gs and stuff it in her slot. She takes it in her hands, turns it lengthwise and feeds it to the counter. Her fingernails are community pool green.

— So, what do you do when you're not banking?

She peers out from under one of her heavily shadowed eyes.

— I spend time with my boyfriend.

— Nice ...

I take a pause and come in on the "two."

— Does he know what to do with you?

It's a pretty insane thing to say to the teller at your bank, and she lets a full measure go by before she responds.

— You know, Mr. Zorn, you are probably a few years older than my father.

— Is that good or bad?

— Perhaps I should get another teller to help you.

— Sorry, I'll behave myself. Sometimes I fall under the illusion that I'm charming, but I appreciate you straightening me out.

— Happy to help.

She gives me a cryptic smile that I could take few different ways and goes about her business. I lower my eyes, looking at a small silver cross lying flat on her pale white chest. It's the only mark on her anywhere.

— How come you don't like compliments?

— Compliments are free.

— You prefer gifts?

— Perhaps. Depends on who's giving them. Is there anything else I can do for you?

— You can let me take you to dinner.

— I just told you I had a boyfriend.

— Well, if he behaves himself he can join us for dessert.

— You are funny.

— Thank you.

— I don't like funny men.

— Me neither, but I just had a momentary streak of good fortune, and I thought it might be nice to celebrate it with someone.

She pauses like only a great actress can.
— Well, I am not that person.
She pushes a white slip through the slot.
— Here is your receipt, Mr. Zorn.
The phrase "you just got your walking papers" appears above my head.

#

I got a headline for all these hip Hollywood production companies. Replace the ping-pong table in the lobby with a couple of people who actually understand story. And Suspicious doesn't just have ping-pong; they also have air hockey, pool, pop-a-shot and two low-slung titanium exercise bikes that look like they were designed by Frank Gehry.

Clearly, I didn't get the memo, because I'm still thinking about things like clarity and character arcs. If I was smart, I'd just bust into Warner Brothers and go, "All right, here it is: 'Jack in the Box, The Movie.' A sad sack Jack in the Box employee enlists the help of a chicken sandwich and curly fries to get his girlfriend back from the school bully, and then once the bully has seen the error of his ways, the two join forces and save the town from aliens by weaponizing the deep fryer and milkshake machine. We even get a third act cameo from Jack himself. The ads for the movie and the ads for the restaurant are interchangeable and work on any platform. After that comes 'Taco Bell, The Sequel'."

#

When I walk in, Wood is squawking on the phone and so far back in his chair I'm scared he's going to flip over.

— There needs to be something that happened in his childhood that makes you understand why he doesn't want to be with a swimsuit model. I think something really good happens if we make her black or blasian ... you ever see that swimsuit model Jarah Mariano ... I wonder if she can act ... Okay we don't have to figure that out now, besides we always can change it all back after we sell it. No, trust me, dude, this is a layup. He's going to start throwing money at us in the room.

I wander over toward the couch and stare at the stack of books on Wood's coffee table. They're all classics, including a first edition of Albert Camus' *The Stranger*. Really smart books on the coffee table, really dumb movies in development. That's how they do it in this town. Wood holds his finger up, letting me know he'll just be a minute, and then gives me a smile that's intended to make me feel that I am somehow part of the deal he's discussing. It's the smile of someone with borderline personality disorder, and if you're looking to be a big producer, more valuable than a great eye for material.

— Hey, I got to scoot, a famous and talented writer just walked into my office ... No, you don't know him, but you know his movies.

I didn't know if the comment made me feel good or bad, but it made me feel something.

— Anyway, make that change, put the treatment into bullet points, and we will go in there and back up the money truck.

He paused, then blasted a laugh like he had just heard the funniest joke of his life from the sexiest woman he'd ever met. He was so far back in his chair it looked like a dental visit.

— Exactly, dude, we're golden.

Wood cantilevered himself back to upright with a lurch, hung up the phone with a spastic lunge, came out from behind his desk and headed toward me. He looked especially expensive and rumpled.

— Where's Nick?

— With his wife at an ultrasound making sure their kid's not deformed.

— That's good, I'd guess you'd want to know if it is.

— I guess. I can't think about kids.

He crashed back down in his chair.

— My projects are my kids.

— Well, they're all deformed.

He laughed hard, but not at my joke.

— So, what's up, what are your big new ideas about the pitch?

— They're not really big new ideas, I just want more rap songs. We need the global reach of hip-hop. I think that particular cultural export is missing from the piece. We need that bullet in our holster.

— Bullets don't go in holsters, guns do.

— You know what I mean.

— Unfortunately.

He smiled, letting me know he was the kind of producer who could take a ribbing.

— Dude, you need to keep hope alive. We're seeing DreamWorks either Tuesday or Wednesday, they're just clearing Jeffrey's schedule, he's getting some environmental award ... or maybe it's for sick children? He's going to buy the pitch, dude. The only thing that still bothers me is our villain.

The villain he was talking about was the Sandman from the Metallica song "Enter Sandman." And he was right, it was the weakest part of the pitch.

— Well, we've talked about that a lot, I can't solve the whole thing perfectly, he's definitely functional, I mean he's not functioning as seamlessly as the Wicked Witch does, but he's serving that purpose, sort of looming over the piece and showing up to remind you there's an overarching danger.

— No, he is. The Sandman's good, he's just not paying off big enough yet. Maybe his powers are so great that he's going to break through the whole jukebox mythology and put the real world in danger. The world outside the jukebox.

— But that's not our movie.

— I know, but that's what I'm saying, we might need something at the end that's a little "not our movie."

— Okay, let me think about that, it could be interesting.

That was my standard answer for an impulsive and ridiculous idea.

— Great, think about it, you're always good at hanging flesh on the bones of my ideas. That's why it's good when we spitball.

If there was a thought bubble over my head it would have said, "Dear God, how has my life come to this?"

— Hey, you got a second? I need to talk to you about something.

He looked at me with a quick lip chew of adrenaline and popped up like hot coffee had been spilled in his lap. He went to the door and cracked it.

— Colleen, hold all my calls, unless it's Ray.

My mind starts racing the second I hear the "hold all calls" alert, maybe they've hit the wall on *Hot Wheels 2* and need to bring in the old master for a "production polish." I'm already deciding whether I should ask for a lump sum or twenty-five grand a week, as Wood crumbles back into his chair and leans forward.

— Dude, what I'm about to tell you has got to stay between just me and you, okay?

— Okay.

— Has to.

— I understand.

— It *has* to.

— Bro, who am I going to tell? If I actually still knew anyone in this town I'd be working.

— Okay, sorry, I just need to be sure.

He took a beat to gather himself but failed miserably.

— Dude ...

He exhaled.

— I relapsed.

I have to admit, that one caught me by surprise.

— Hey man, it happens. You're an alcoholic, alcoholics drink.

— No dude, I'm talking about a *real* relapse. Pills, booze, coke ... snorting Ritalin ... I even did some ketamine the other day ...

— Ketamine? For real?

He nodded his eyes.

— You ever done it?

— No. I'll do horse but not horse tranquilizer.

— Dude I went so deep into a k-hole I thought I'd never climb out. I accomplished more spiritual growth in six hours than you can with a lifetime of meditation.

he wasn't just high on the drugs; he was high on the relapse, and had that twisted mixture of excitement an addict feels when he's in the process of blowing up his life.

— What are you going to do?

— I don't know. Stop, I guess.

He rocked forward, ran his hands through his sweat-greased hair.

— Dude, I'm *so* much better at this job high. The second I stop giving a fuck everything just starts going my way.

There it was, the official Buddhist lesson for the day.

— I know I have to get my ass to a meeting, but I don't want to stop.

He looked at me like we had known each other since first grade.

— Dude, you're the only person I've told. The only people who know are you and the two women I've got living with me.

— The Russian ones?

— Yeah, how do you know about them?

— You talked about them at DreamWorks. You told that whole story about taking them to Mexico.

— Did I? I don't even remember that, I was so gakked on Ritalin.

A physical sensation comes over me like I'm shrink-wrapped from the waist up. I try to see him as an addict who fucked up, but he isn't an addict who fucked up, he's my producer, my producer who I've been working for, for free, for months, and now, a few days before our winner-take-all match with Katzenberg, he's decided to dive into a k-hole and swim for it.

— Dude, you're an addict, you can't use. I mean, you can use, but it's not going to end well.

— I know, dude. That's why I'm telling you. I want to go to a meeting, just not today.

He was now behind his desk rummaging through a drawer.

— What happened, man, you were out, and a drink just sounded good to you?

— No, it was a medical thing, I cracked a tooth on a chicken wing, and my dentist was out of town, so I went and saw Owen Wilson's dentist, and she was like, "Do you want a few Vicodin just in case?" and I was like, "Okay, just in case." I ate four before I had even gotten on the elevator.

— Water?

He shook his head, then put his flat palm beneath his chin, and pantomimed throwing four pills down his gullet. I could feel the big, chalky ovals in my throat.

— That was two weeks ago, I've been off and running ever since.

I stared off and tried to get my head around the situation. Maybe I was overreacting, I mean, fuck, I had had ninety-five percent of my success while I was using. This might be exactly what the project needed.

— Don't worry about the meeting with DreamWorks, we're going to kill it.

When I looked back up he was coming right at me, a small sheet of aluminum foil in one hand, and a rolled-up aluminum foil straw in the other. He sat down across from me, his forehead scrunched with purpose.

— You're smoking heroin?

— Have to, it's really tough to get pills these days, the way they're watching doctors.

He dug a lighter out of his pocket.

— Bro, don't smoke that shit in front of me!

— I'm really bad at this. I lose like half the smoke.

If I had any sense I'd run out of the room like it was a burning building, but instead, I just sit there and watch as he puts the straw in his mouth and some flame to the bottom of the blackened foil. When that sweet, burnt vinegar smell hits my nose I have to do everything in my power not to throw up all over Camus.

— I keep missing it.

— That's 'cause you're sucking too hard, just do it easy, and tilt the foil more, so it comes toward you, you don't really "chase" it.

I probably shouldn't have been schooling him in the art of proper heroin smoking, but I can't stand watching an amateur. Wood tilts the foil down a little more, and I see the lump of dope on it. It's half the size of a pencil eraser, and the color of buckwheat honey. He hits the lighter again, and the lump hisses and skids. When I smell it this time I actually do puke a little in my mouth.

I jump up and rush out of the room with the taste of my guts on my tongue. When I get out into the parking lot, I'm shaken. For a couple of years now I've been convinced that shit no longer has any pull on me whatsoever, and that I haven't just stopped using it, I've outgrown it. But when the smell of that black tar hit my nose, all that went flying out the window, and I was left defenseless, like a little eight-year-old face-to-face with his abuser. Only my abuser was me.

18.

It's been burning a hole in my pocket ever since Malibu. I've neglected it, looked to get around it, even straight-up tried to ignore it, but it doesn't want to be ignored. What's actually in my pocket is just an iPhone, the new appendage of the twenty-first century, what's burning the hole is a number on that phone, and that number belongs to Kyle Strange.

Must have been about a year and a half ago. I was living on fumes, writing a web series about a homeless soccer team. I'm on the phone with the producer arguing about whether the right wing lives in a tent or refrigerator box when "call waiting" clicks in. It's Kyle. I ignore it, but he clicks in again, and then again. Three successive calls from a struggling junkie on a Sunday afternoon—I wouldn't call that a good sign. I tell the producer I'll call him back. Sometimes AA responsibilities even come before great art.

— Did you mean to call three times or is it a pocket dial calamity?

— Dude, I need you to come get me. A guy just bet me a thousand dollars I can't shoot an eight ball of coke in an hour.

— He's right, you can't.

— I'm serious, man, you got to get me out of here, everywhere I look there's white or brown.

— I thought you were going to the noon meeting?

— I was, but Lupita called and said she needed to talk, so I met her in Chinatown.

Lupita was Kyle's ex, a charming but scandalous junkie who somehow still had all her teeth.

— I thought you blocked her number.

— I did, but I unblocked it.

I was ready to admonish him strongly but realized I had done the same thing with three different women within the last month. Though none of them liked to shoot smack in their neck.

— You got to come get me. Lupita drove, and now she's locked in the bathroom smoking crack.

— Dude, take the fucking bus, you'd take it to cop, so take it to not cop.

— Bobby, please. If I stay here I'm gonna get high, and I have to test for my PO tomorrow.

PO stood for parole officer.

— I thought you tested for him last week.

— No, it's tomorrow. Please man, I'm scared.

He was lying about the parole officer, but clearly not about being scared.

— Why did you get in the car with her? You know what happens when you two get together.

— I know, dude, I think I'm just cursed. It's like I've got a hex on me or a demon or something.

— Did you already do a shot?

— No.

— Tell me the fucking truth.

— I haven't.

— But some guy wants you to shoot an eight ball?

— Just come and get me, please. I don't want to be this person anymore, I just want to paint and draw.

— Dude, just take Lupita's keys and get the fuck out of there.

— I can't. She's locked up in the bathroom with a bunch of rocks. You gotta come get me.

Now, the unspoken rule in Alcoholics Anonymous is that you "never turn down an AA request," which means if someone asks you to speak at a meeting or on a panel at a rehab, you always say yes, though less than half the sober folks I know actually follow the protocol. But when a struggling alcoholic or junkie calls and says: I'm staring at a pile of coke and the chick who drove me here is holed up in the john with a crack pipe in her mouth, you put down whatever you're doing and go do your fucking duty, even if you can't stand the motherfucker, which was the opposite of how I felt about Kyle.

— Please man, please, I don't want this life anymore.

— All right dude, I'll come, where are you?

— Compton.

— What?! You're in fucking Compton, what the fuck, dude? I'm in Woodland Hills, it'll take me an hour to get there.

— No, it won't, it's Sunday, there's no traffic.

— I got to take the 101 through downtown. There's always traffic.

— Just come, I'll wait for you.

— With a pile of coke in your face? Just get the fuck out of there!

— I'm in *Compton*. Where am I gonna go?

— Just go to a McDonald's or something, I'll pick you up there.

— No, I can't.

— Why?

— Because he won't let me.

— Who won't let you?

— This Crip.

— What Crip?

— This OG Crip I'm with.

— Why are you with an OG Crip?

— He's a friend of Lupita's.

— The dude she lived with in high school, who strangled the pit bull?

— Yeah, Buddha ... He didn't strangle it, he *stabbed* it. He's not gonna let me leave.

— Why not?

— Because I bet him about the coke.

— Well, tell him the bet's off.

— Why do I have this demon in me? I need an exorcism. Bobby, you got to help me, there's not even running water in this place, they made me draw up the water from a dirty toilet.

— I thought you hadn't shot anything yet.

— I did one.

— Just coke?

— Yeah.

— No wonder you're freaking out.

— I had sixty-eight days, and I fucking threw it away, I'm really sorry, man.

— Dude, I don't care about your sixty-eight days, I care about you getting out of there alive.

— My heart is pounding really hard.

— Well, do a shot of junk so you can calm the fuck down and think clearly.

— You're telling me to shoot dope.

— Dude, you already fucked up, that ship sailed, do some fucking dope and get your head on straight. You do a big shot of coke on its own, what are you a fucking lunatic?

— They're not gonna let me shoot dope with the coke, that was part of the bet. They're gonna make me shoot this coke. They're gonna force me!

I don't know how much coke he had really shot, but he sounded halfway to the madhouse.

— Kyle, listen to me, you just got a bunch of coke in you so you're freaking out. Just get your ass out of there. Go to a 7-Eleven, and I'll come get you.

— It's not like that, man, there's like ten dudes here.

— I thought it was just Buddha?

— No, there's like ten guys from his set here.

— What set?

— Spook Town Compton Crips.

— Are you serious, that's their fucking name?

— Yeah. Buddha's uncle founded them.

I heard a banging noise, like someone pounding on a door, then a deep muffled voice, then Kyle saying, "Okay, I'm just talking to my mom." It was a sharp play. If you want some old banger to give you a minute, tell him you're talking to your mom.

— Dude, please, just come.

— Where are you?

— I'm in a little storage room.

— No, dude, where in Compton?

— Some storefront on Alondra Boulevard.

— Where?

— I'm not sure.

— Bro, what's the fucking address? I can't just start driving up and down Alondra Boulevard looking for storefronts.

— It's near a Church's fried chicken.

— I'll bet it is.

— Bobby, please, just get me out of here. I'll do anything, I'll start going to the Pacific Group.

— Dude, shut the fuck up and just listen to me.

— I'm freaking out.

— Kyle.

— Dude, they're gonna kill me.

— No, they're not.

— They're gonna kill me.

— Dude, you're fucking white, they're not going to kill you. Now, calm down, shut the fuck up, and listen to me.

I gave him a second to get his shit together.

— I want you to go back in there and I want you to walk up to this Buddha cat and say, "Look, man, I am a terrible fucking drug addict, and I don't know why I bet you I could shoot an eight ball of coke in an hour, but I'm trying to live a decent fucking life, and I can't shoot drugs because it's killing me, and I'm sorry that I said I could, but I got to get out of here now." And dude, I promise you, he's going let you go, because all he sees is struggling addicts, and he's probably been waiting for his mother or father to say that to him his whole life. So just go in there and do that, and get your ass somewhere safe and public, and I will be there as quickly as I can.

— I can't do that.

— Why not?

— Because I can't leave Lupita.

— Dude, Lupita can take care of herself.

— No, she can't.

— Kyle, you can't help Lupita, she's a horrible fucking junkie, and she doesn't want to be clean, we've had this conversation a hundred times.

— I love her.

— No, you don't, you love the pain she causes you because you know it and it's comfortable. Look, let's not get into this right now. Just go in there and say what I told you to, and *get the fuck out of there*.

— I'm not leaving Lupita.

— So, what, you want me to come to a storefront dope house in Compton and help you get Lupita out of the bathroom and past a room full of Crips?

— Yes.

— Kyle, you can't save Lupita. Now you can either save yourself, or you can go down with her.

— I can't leave her here.

— You know what, dude, you're right. You do have a demon in you.

I hung up the phone and called my sponsor. He said what I knew he'd say, that I couldn't go down there alone, and that Kyle had his own higher power and it would look out for him. It was the kind of party-line doctrinaire bullshit that made me hate AA.

I texted Kyle and told him that if he left and got somewhere, I'd come get him, but I didn't hear back. I called and texted every day for the next two weeks, but all I got was silence.

His sister had heard from him, so I knew he wasn't dead. Then about a month later I saw him at the same Alvarado meeting where we had met. I went up to him with my best guilty smile and said, "You're a tough dude to get in touch with." He didn't smile back. "I've got a new sponsor and he says I shouldn't have anything to do with you anymore, so please just leave me alone."

It felt like a knife in the stomach. I hadn't had any contact with him since. I dig my phone out and look for his number. Any sane person would have just called him right away, but I'm scared he's going to see who it is and ignore the call or worse, block me like Carla did. He probably already has.

There's three contacts for him (junkies can never keep their phones on): "Kyle S," "Kyle 2014," and "Newest Kyle." I don't know whether to call or text. I decide to rip the Band-Aid off fast and call. Now, I can either be real casual and just see if he wants to "catch up" over coffee, or I can just come out and go "so what happened with Carla? Because her sister says this and her brother says that, and what do you know about this bag, this ring, these drawings, and by the way, I'm real sorry about what happened, but can you please explain to me what the fuck could she have possibly seen in you?"

I hit the number for "Newest Kyle," and it doesn't even ring, just goes right to that three-tone, old-school, phone-company recording, "The number you have called is no longer in service, please check the number and dial again." There's relief in the disappointment, and disappointment in the relief.

19.

When you cross Olympic, Wilton turns into Arlington, when you cross Jefferson, it turns into something else. I hit Western, turn south, and pass the KFC where I'd meet Robert Lee near the end. He'd get me a handful of sad eight-dollar balloons when my steady Mexican was closed for the night. It's the same shopping center where Mac's barbershop was, and where Silver's wheelchair got hit by a city bus. That's how it is down here, every corner has a story, and every story has four more stories that come along with it.

The fast food joints fade, and the street becomes a patchwork of battered churches and liquor stores. South Central as a whole has steadily gone from black to brown, but this part of Western's still got that "you buy we fry" feel to it. I roll past Ray of Light Baptist, then come up on the Barack Obama Global Preparation Academy, which sounds like a diplomatic think tank, but is really just a middle school. I hit a red light on 39th, and a loping black dude in a nylon wife-beater crosses my windshield. He's wrangling a hard-faced white girl, screaming in her pitted grill, "Well, you ain't gettin' no bacon in your breakfast burrito, bitch!"

I could explain my theories on why South Central and particularly black South Central is so raging, bipolar crazy, but it would take too much time. But the overall message down here is: You motherfuckers are on your own. We don't care, and we never did, so don't call, don't write, and please don't bother us unless you've figured out a way to turn that good, ghetto otherness into something we can sell. There's also the fact that half the block is on disability, SSI or General Relief, so you got 50 percent of the population living on bimonthly checks, which means they act rich for three days, then are dead broke for the next eleven. Fifty years of that and the whole neighborhood turns full-blown schizophrenic.

#

The grounds of the Snooty Fox Motor Inn are nicely landscaped, and for a place where the clientele comes to shoot dope, smoke coke, and turn tricks, it's downright tropical. A Latino security guard with an official brown uniform and an even more official brown mustache oversees matters from a football-field-sized parking lot. I throw him an un-returned nod, and head for the front desk, which at the Snooty is a walk-up booth like you find at a twenty-four-hour gas station, only the Plexiglas window is completely, and I mean totally, blacked out. They can see you, but you can't see anything.

I get in line behind a hardworking mid-forties sister with a bad weave, and a big Chairman Mao mole on her chin. She's wearing a lumpy, magenta leotard as only a wasted fifty-year-old hooker can. I hang back, and make sure to give her plenty of room. It's best to follow "penitentiary rules" at a place like this, which means you don't watch me when I work my hustle, and I won't watch you when you work yours. I learned that the hard way when I was too curious about an old junkie on line at the methadone clinic as he "gummed" his dose. He waited for me outside and let me know he didn't appreciate the attention.

— Let me get three hours, baby.

That's what she tells the black glass in a honey-soaked whisper. If she can talk that nice to a slab of black plastic, imagine what she can do if she looks you in the eye. I can't hear the voice on the other side, but she pulls out a few crumpled bills and puts them in the stainless-steel drawer like she's buying a few gallons of unleaded. She takes her card key, and waddles off in her flip-flops, each toenail a customized work of art.

Now it's my turn. My play is to tell him the last time I was here, my girl left her bag, and I was hoping it might be in the lost and found. It's a long shot that it's there or that the wallet would still be in it if it was, but for the moment it's the best I got.

I step up to the black slab, and just stand there, unsure who's supposed to talk first.

— Can I help you?

The voice is a lot deeper than I'm expecting, and through the cheap drive-through-style squawk box, sounds like a ghetto Wizard of Oz.

— Um … can I look at a room?

There goes my plan.

— Look at it how?

— Well, I just want to see a room, so I can make sure it works for what I have planned.

He doesn't answer right away, and I can feel him looking at me thinking to himself what the fuck is this white boy up to? Or maybe that's what I'm thinking. But then he's back.

— All right, hold on a minute.

I nod to the black nothingness and wait. My mind starts racing. I can still ask about the lost and found after I see the room, but if I've lost something, that means I've been there before, and already know what the rooms look like, so why am I asking to see a room unless I want to see a different room, and then I should just say "I was here once before, but the room I had wasn't to my liking and I was hoping I could see a different one."

It's already been about a minute when I turn around and nod again at the security guard. He still won't play along. I glance down at the south wing and wonder how many of the people in those rooms are fixing at this very moment. I mean actually pushing down the plunger right now. It's probably not the healthiest thing to be contemplating, considering that I had the smell of dope in my nose an hour ago.

— Just need a driver's license.

A metal drawer comes forward. I fish out my wallet and drop my license in it. The drawer disappears then reemerges with a card key.

— Room 208 at the south end.

I pick up the card key and thank the faceless Oz voice behind the black glass. As I walk past the security guard I keep my eyes straight ahead. He nods to me.

#

Room 208 is half Motel 6, half Playboy Mansion. The focal point is a king size bed with a purple faux velvet bedspread. This sits on top of a shit brown shag carpet with enough human DNA in it to keep a geneticist happy for a hundred years. Behind the bed is a cutout with a big mirror. Directly over the bed is another big mirror, but this one is round and convex, curving down like a giant reflective tit. I think its purpose is to make you look skinnier, but I'm not curious enough to hop up on the bed and find out. To the left is another cutout with another big mirror. There's no escape. If your plan is to smoke crack and cheat on your wife with a sixteen-year-old Salvadorian waitress, you're going to have to watch yourself do it from more angles than a Michael Bay movie.

There's got to be over a hundred rooms in this place, so the chances are slim that this is the one Carla died in, but I decide to check the bathroom anyway. I step around the corner and there isn't even a door, just an open space almost as big as the room. The whole thing's done in a shiny aqua tile. The effect is more locker room than honeymoon. There's double sinks on one side, and a huge, curtainless open shower against the back wall, so if Carla really died in a bathtub, she didn't die here.

I close the door behind me, and there's a Latina housekeeper on the walkway with her cart. She gives me a tight smile, and I nod a smile back, then head down the walkway wondering how to present my lost-and-found case to the voice behind the plastic. I get an impulse to turn around.

— Excuse me Senora, *tengo una pregunta, por favor.*

I'm pretty sure I've told her I have a question, but I can never be sure.

— What is it?

So much for my gringo Spanish.

— A few weeks ago a girl, a friend of mine, died here. It would mean a lot to me if I could go to that room and pay my respects.

She looks at me with kindness, and like she doesn't believe a word of it.

— I don't know.

— You don't know if you can or you don't know which room?

I could have found out which room from a police report, but I was keeping clear of the cops for Kyle's sake ... And because cops make me nervous.

— I don't know.

— You must have heard about it, it was just a few weeks ago ... She was found in a bathtub, she was a very beautiful girl, and she was a dear, dear friend of mine ... All I want is to be close to her spirit for a moment, you know, to her *alma.*

When I said *alma* I could see her soften just a little bit.

— No. I am sorry for your loss, I cannot help you with this.

I give her the sweetest, sweetheart, Jew-boy eyes I have. She's appreciative, but not transformed.

— I'm sorry, I must work now.

She reaches to her cart for a clear spray bottle full of a Windex-blue liquid, and I notice a well-read book next to it. It's black, and the gold lettering on the cover says, "New World Translations of the Holy Scriptures."

— Are you a Jehovah's Witness?

She looks up at me like I'm treading where I shouldn't.

— Yes, why?

— I just saw the Bible.

— Oh.

She does a little something with the corners of her mouth and goes back to her supplies.

— Do you know a woman named Elsa?

She pauses, then comes up from behind her cart and meets my eyes.

— Which Elsa?

— Elsa who's married to Oskar.

That puts an even bigger pause into her than the Jehovah's Witness question.

— Yes. I know her.

— Do you belong to the same congregation?

She doesn't answer but her eyes do.

— Do you remember a little boy they used to bring with them, a little white boy with blue eyes, a little pudgy? They brought him all the time.

Her eyes answer for her again.

— That's my son.

She looks at me like she wants me to be making it up but knows I'm not.

— Stanlito is your son?

— Yes, Stanlito is my son. Elsa used to work for us back in the day. Here, this is what he looks like now.

I take out my phone and show her a recent picture. A smile comes to her eyes.

— Such a beautiful boy. Ask him if he remembers Rena.

#

The room where Carla died was on the first floor. Room 126. We had to walk past the front desk, and I had absolutely no idea if the man behind the plastic was watching us or not. Rena had left her cart behind, and we moved along in silence. With the tropical setting and her magnificent black hair, it was almost like we were out for a Sunday stroll.

She pulls out her pass key and opens the door.

— I will leave you to your friend.

She closes it behind me. It's like she's closing the door to a vault. I give a quick look around, the room stays true to theme, only in this one the bedspread's crimson, and the mirror above is square, not round. And then my throat tightens, and it hits me like a whiff of ammonia, like I'm about to have a stroke. But what I smell isn't burnt almonds; it's the hot radiation of depravity. It's like fucking Los Alamos in here and I can feel every dark deed that ever went down between these walls. Every shot, every trick, every suicide installment, every sordid deed and savage act of self-violence: every grunt, groan, bite mark and bitch-slap, every weeping abscess and wounded child. I can feel the doom of every shame-sick desperado who's ever tried to live their life one paid hour at a time.

I stumble into the bathroom expecting the worst, but something about the aqua tiles cools my brain. I look over at the toilet. It's pastel pool green, with stainless steel hospital handrails on either side, just in case you shit your liver out and need to hold on for dear life. I look over to the left and there it is, a simple white tub like an empty grave. But no cross or placard. Nothing to mark that twenty days ago a lost and heartsick girl chose this modest spot to lay down her hand and get up from the table. God-dammit, Kyle, what did you do? Did you nod out and come up too late, or did you run out for a pack of smokes, return to her blue and breathless? Was it a mistake, a bad batch? Was there puke bubbling out of her nose and mouth, did you run to the ice machine and try to shove cubes up her ass to bring her back, did you sob over her like a bad movie, or did you just grab her bag and bolt, and toss the whole dark tale into the backseat like an empty beer can, and keep on driving? What happened, and where's that wallet, and why do you have to be such a junkie disaster that you can't even keep your phone on for more than a week? Jesus fucking Christ, dude, can't you just shoot dope like a gentleman?

#

The lost and found is where they keep the bedding, but as opposed to a linen closet, it's a linen stadium. There's two of the biggest washing machines I've ever seen in my life, but there's no soap strong enough to wash out the shame that's in those sheets and towels. I had told Rena that my friend might have left a bag, and that maybe it ended up in the lost and found.

— Anything in it of value will no longer be inside.

I said I figured but wanted to check anyway. She nodded and offered me her warm, brown gaze to do with as I wished.

On the way to the sheets she informed me that it was her friend who had found Carla, but that according to her, the tub had no water in it, and that Carla was in just her choneys and a tiny shirt. When she said it, I got a lump in my throat, and the dark weight of Carla's death finally hit me for the first time. Sometimes it takes a second story to make the first story real.

— I don't think she would get into an empty bathtub in her choneys, so maybe someone put her there.

It was a solid piece of deduction on my part, but then again, trying to make sense of a speed-balling junkie's behavior was a losing proposition. To be perfectly honest, shooting up in an empty bathtub in your underwear kinda made sense to me; you wouldn't get blood on your clothes, your ass and back wouldn't get cold against the porcelain, and if you couldn't find a vein, you could peel off your undies, fill up the tub with hot water, and bring a few out.

#

The actual "lost and found" is a large appliance box cut in half. It has all kinds of crap in it: Mardi Gras beads, a bunch of crusty curling irons, an even more crusty old Osterizer blender, a series of leashes and dog toys intended use unknown, a rice cooker, a very dirty taffeta wedding dress, a small Sylvania black-and-white TV with a cracked screen, and a bunch of books, mostly kid books, so little junior can sit in the bathroom with Curious George, as mom slips a condom on some "nice man's" cock with her mouth. But what really grabs my attention is an old prosthetic leg. Looks like something out of a David Lynch movie. It's got a hanging strap that goes around the waist like a belt, and a two-tone brown sock painted on it from calf to ankle. At the bottom of that is a very nice though well-worn burgundy wing-tip shoe, the laces still tied in a fifty-year-old bow. Now, I understand how you could be so high or fuck-drunk that you leave behind the phone charger, but walking out without your leg strikes me as especially forgetful.

I dig through the box some more, pulling my sleeves over like mittens and using the backs of my hands. There's no handbag, much less a handbag with a fancy Italian wallet still inside.

— This is the only lost and found?

— Yes, there is a box at the front desk, but it is full of only charging cords for phones.

— Do you know how soon the police came?

— A few hours at least. When there is trouble here they first try to take care of it on their own.

— Is there a lot of trouble here?

— Not as much as you would think.

I go back to the box just for the hell of it and nudge a deflated *Finding Nemo* pool toy out of the way. Then something catches my eye. It isn't a bag or a wallet, it's an old yellow-brown Pee-Chee school folder with the '50s retro-style drawings of athletes on the cover. It's similar to the one I had my pitch document in at DreamWorks. I had given one to Kyle with a copy of the "fourth step" out of the Narcotics Anonymous workbook inside. He never did the work, but he dug the folder and started carrying his sketches in it.

I pull the Pee-Chee out and flip it over. There's my dyslexic, lefty scrawl. I had written "work for Kyle to not do." I was trying AA reverse psychology, but like any good junkie he was immune to it. I open the folder and find a series of sketches. The first one's of a cigarette lighter lying alone on a table next to a filled ashtray, and it just about breaks my heart. The next one is the parking lot and palm trees as seen from out the window, a bit of curtain in foreground. It's accurate and Hitchcock-skewed at the same time. The next sketches are of Carla on the bed in her underwear. They're so pure and tender they knock your head off. He's got her. What I wished I could capture in words he's got with charcoal, only he knows her in a way I never will. The last one is of her sleeping on her side from the shoulders up, her hands flat together under her cheek like a child at nap time. He had finished her eyes and nose, but only half of her mouth.

— Is that your friend?

Rena was next to me, looking over my shoulder.

— Yeah, another friend of mine drew it.

She stared at the unfinished sketch.

— He really loved her.

20.

When I got out of the hospital after the heart surgery and bleeding ulcer ordeal, I was on 180 milligrams of methadone, more than twice as much as is given to terminal patients in the final days of hospice. I was gutted, bloated, and soaked through with synthetic opiates. My doctors hadn't agreed on much except one thing: the fact that I was alive was a miracle. I was a physical wreck, and as for my career prospects, I had lost whatever I'd had, and anything I might get in the future. It was over. I was broke, broken and beyond reprieve. I had resigned myself to wandering the 99 Cent Store in sandals and socks, like a mental patient. I started going to AA meetings 'cause I had nothing else to do.

At my first meeting, the woman sitting next to me asked if I had had brain surgery. It was far from encouraging. But I didn't give up. I kept going, and over four years and about two thousand meetings I steadily decreased the 'done, getting myself all the way down from 180 milligrams to 10. I checked into Brotman Detox, a place I had been tossed out of three times (twice for using in my room and once for physically threatening a doctor) to get off that. I went from ten to zero in a week. When I came home I was opiate-free for the first time in twenty years. It was insane. I felt like I was on another planet. Going cold turkey off heroin is a hysterical four-day exorcism, but doing it off methadone is a six-week diesel grind. The aches and pains were deep, thudding, and *relentless*. I didn't sleep more than an hour a night for a month. My only recourse was to drag myself on long pre-dawn walks and plead with my body to produce its own endorphins.

But as brutal as it was, there was something incredibly freeing about it. In fact, I had never felt so alive. When I wasn't walking I listened to *Blood on the Tracks* on repeat, wrote simple rhyming poetry and wept from grief and joy. It was baptismal. I, Robert Zorn, had gone full phoenix and somehow risen from the ashes. And now, here I was a few years later, ready to flush it all down the toilet just to be near a girl. A strung-out girl ... A strung-out girl who was coming to whisk me away in an hour with dope in her pocket.

I packed a small bag and even brought along some good out-loud reading material of the inspirational variety. I'm not really sure what happened next. I just remember the room getting wobbly. I must have had some kind of seizure 'cause when I came to a few minutes later I had actually shat my pants. My body was doing for me what my brain couldn't.

I called my sponsor. He taught a directing class at LMU two nights a week, but I could never remember which nights. If he answered, I'd tell him what I was planning to do and see what he said. If not, it was smooth sailing.

Turned out he taught on Monday and Wednesday. This was a Thursday. He picked up on the first ring.

— Hey Jimmy, it's me man. I got a little situation on my hands.

— Okay, shoot?

— You know that girl Carla? Who Pamela E. used to sponsor?

He laughed a very specific kind of laugh and said "What about her?"

— She's strung out again and she wants me to help her kick. She's on her way over here to pick me up and take me down to the desert for a week and she's got dope in her pocket for the first night, and I'm not sure what to do.

He was sure. Very. It was a short call.

I called Carla as soon as I hung up with him. She was in the car.

— Gower is east of Western or west of Western?

— Two blocks west; listen, I have to talk to you.

— Okay, but first I have to talk to you, what kind of snacks do you like, sweet or salty or both?

— I can't go with you tonight.

I waited for a response but there wasn't any.

— Look, I'll help you, I'll do anything for you. I'll get you into a place, I'll drive you there, I'll visit you every day, I'll take you to meetings when you get out, but I can't go help you kick somewhere just me and you.

More silence.

— One of my best friends runs a rehab in the Valley. It's not like Promises or that fancy place up on Mulholland you went to. It's got real people in it. You'll love this guy, he hates AA. Go there for thirty days, and I will come every single day, and I don't care what your sister says or anybody else.

Nothing, just the faint sound of the radio ...

— I'm really sorry, but it's just not something I can do.

— What's the name of the place your friend runs?

— I forget, it's in Reseda, but it's a good place, and he's amazing.

— Okay, call him.

— You'll go.

— I don't know.

— Okay. Let me call and see if there's a bed for you, and you can talk to him. I'll call you right back.

I hung up and called my friend TJ. He didn't answer so I texted him. In ten minutes he texted me back "Have her call me." I called Carla to tell her, but her phone picked up without ringing. I tried again, same thing. Then I texted her TJ's number. It didn't go through. I kept trying to call her for an hour hoping maybe her phone had died, but it wasn't that. She had blocked me. I didn't know what to do with myself. I was scared she would call Angie and tell her or that she'd be so undone by my change of heart that she'd just say "fuck it" and go on some crazy run that would do her in, in a week, but I was wrong on two fronts. I was the one completely undone, and it took her two years to die.

21.

Beverly Hills always gives me a feeling of low-grade doom. I cross Rodeo, and spy the Beverly Wilshire Hotel, a squat yet elegant white brick vault of a building. Sixty years ago, you might find Tennessee Williams in the lobby, eyeing the bellhops, considering who to cast in *Cat on a Hot Tin Roof*. Now it's just YouTube stars taking pictures of their breakfast. The only thing left around here that's still good is the Beverly Hills Cheese Store, and it's closed. Too bad, I could have used a quick whiff to clear my head.

I pull over in front of the City National Bank and sit a minute, still hollowed out by my field trip to the Snooty. I take out my phone and reread the e-mail that's brought me west of La Cienega.

"I'm sitting in my little yard, taking blissful breaths of hibiscus and lavender, and remembering that everything is transient and imperfect. Do you know *wabi-sabi*, the Japanese aesthetic of embracing imperfection? I built my garden around that principle, but I must say, with a good cup of tea in my lap and Chagall at my feet, things are pretty damned close to perfect. All that being said, I feel I may not have been completely forthright with you about something, Bobby, and it's gnawing at me. I have to show my face at an opening tonight, in Beverly Hills of all places, and I was hoping we could meet there. The artist is Important, so that's a perk. Can you do eight o'clock at the Barkasian Gallery on Camden? XOXO Angie."

#

The sound meets me from forty feet away, and the treble is up high, as it always is when the crowd is rich and white. I walk in and some clay-colored dude nods at me. He's straddling the line between security guard and fashion model, and sets the mood with his Italian black suit and Secret Service earpiece. There are rackets, and there are *rackets*; separating rich folks from their dough in the name of art is one of the best.

The Barkasian Gallery is a vast white-walled pen with a slab concrete floor buffed to the gloss of a Harlem pimp's fingernails. Above all this textureless minimalism is a rounded, wood ceiling with crisscross planks cut into it, so it's nothing but texture. The cumulative effect is just hip and rarified enough to make some Johnny Hedge Fund feel his artistic oats and whip out his checkbook.

As for the paintings, they're big, sprawling splotches of color, but they don't pack the wallop those sketches in the Pee-Chee do. I'm lost in a gash of blue when the high cackling laugh of privilege hits me like a champagne bottle to the head. I look over and two bejeweled opera ladies are all a titter about something. I'd bet the five grand Liam gave me that they smell just like my Aunt Bobby did when she hugged me on Passover. I'm a long way from the Barack Obama Global Preparation Academy—that's for damn sure.

I look across the room, and there's Angie, tucked in a corner, and looking right at home. She's with some European type whose salt-and-pepper hair alone looks like it's worth a half billion.

— What's going on?

I came in from the flank and caught her by surprise.

— My God, Bobby, where did you come from?

— I blew in from your *wabi-sabi* daydream.

— Well, that's a very weird thing to say, but okay.

I didn't understand what was weird about it since I was referencing her e-mail, but I guess normal people don't remember every word they write.

— Bobby, this is Geronimo Pucci.

I kept my hand in my pocket and gave him my best I-don't-give-a-shit nod, but he didn't take the bait, and hit me back with a high-thread-count smile.

— Geronimo's a dear friend.

— Nice.

He added some twinkling brown eyes to the smile.

— That's a pretty strong moniker you got there, brother. You named after the Indian chief?

— Yes, actually. My father was obsessed with Native Americans.

— Well then, you're lucky. He could have named you Sitting Bull.

Angie was undecided about the comment, but luckily Geronimo laughed.

— Are you liking the show, sweetie?

— Yeah, it's swell.

— I can't tell if you're being serious or facetious?

— Luckily there's not much difference.

I smiled at Geronimo to let him know I was a hip and cryptic cat, but my thread count was down in the 200s.

— Go look at the rest of the show. I need about twenty minutes to bow and scrape before some people it's good for me to bow and scrape before.

— I don't got twenty minutes.

She looked at me like I was speaking Arabic.

— Well, I at least need a moment to finish up with Gerry.

— No, no, it is fine, do what you need to do.

Geronimo gave her a quick kiss on the cheek, hit me a parting nod, and was gone.

— That was rather rude.

— Something tells me he'll be okay.

— I meant to me.

— Yeah, well something tells me you'll be okay too.

— My, my, what's gotten into you?

— Nothing, I have showed up in Beverly Hills just like you asked.

— That was very thoughtful of you.

— Well, I'm a very thoughtful boy.

— Did you get a chance to see the work?

— I took a few peeks.

— What do you think?

— I think Mark Rothko should get residual checks.

— Really? I think if she's leaning on anyone, it's Pollack.

— You'd know better than me.

— I appreciate that, sweetie, but there really isn't anything to know, it's all so painfully subjective.

— It sure is. Painfully. So, what do you want to talk to me about?

— We'll dip into that in a moment, but first tell me, have you had any success locating this boy?

— Not yet, but I'm into it.

I should have just come out and said, "Yeah, I'm looking for him, but for your brother, not you."

— I went down to the Snooty Fox today and had a look around.

That made her lean forward like people do when the movie gets good.

— Did you find anything out?

— Yeah, I found out there's a lot of sad people in the world doing a lot of strange shit to deal with it.

— Well, you already knew that, didn't you?

— I did, but it's always good to be reminded. Guess some folks like to get up to no good down on Western, and some like to buy million-dollar paintings on Camden Drive.

She gave me a haughty little smile that was meant for a different kind of man.

— I don't think this crowd is quite as sad as that one.

— I think they're sadder.

— My, my, you really are in a mood, aren't you?

— Yeah, maybe I am. Now, what do you want to tell me?

— You have no solid leads on this boy?

— I told you I'm looking for him, and why do you keep calling him a boy? He's a thirty-five-year-old dude who was with your sister. Now come on, tell me what's up. What little piece of Angie-ness did I have to come all the way past Doheny for?

Her jaw tightened, but before she could answer, some old dowager caught her eye, and she squeezed off a stiff smile. When she came back around, her blue eyes were hissing.

— There's something very dark about you tonight, Bobby, and it doesn't feel like play.

— Does that mean you're not going to take me to Italy?

She shot me a look like she hated my guts. It was the first time she looked sexy all night.

— You know I was actually quite serious about that, but now I realize you'll need to ruin it like you ruin everything else. Now, did you find anything out at that motel?

— Yeah. Your sister's dead and you're not.

Her face went white.

— My God, you really do say some horrible things.

— Here, take this back.

I reached down into my pocket and pulled out the five hundred dollars.

— I don't think I can do this job for you.

— What are you talking about?

— I can't do it. I'm done.

— You said you'd find this boy for me.

— Yeah, well, I changed my mind.

I held out the money, as if I wasn't just rejecting her dough, but

the entire idea of her.
— What is going on with you?
— Nothing's going on with me.
— Then why are you acting like this?
— What do you want to tell me?
— It doesn't matter anymore.
— Your e-mail said you haven't been forthright about something; what is it?
— Why? Clearly, you've made some decision about all this without knowing a bloody thing.
— Well, tell me what's going on, and maybe I'll change my decision.
— I'm not going to tell you anything if you're going to throw my money back at me like you don't even know me.
— Look, Kyle's a real person, okay, he's not some stringy-haired junkie with a needle in one hand and your sister's bag in the other. He was there with her when she died, while you were up in Malibu feeding your dog.
— And what, that's a good thing? That he was with her in some hellish hotel room, helping her kill herself?
— It's a real thing. Would it have been better for you if she died alone?
— It would have been better if she hadn't died at all. Now, are you going to do what you said or are you going to stay true to form and let me down yet again?
I felt a high fastball of shame whiz by, and I had to struggle not to swing at it.
— This isn't just a chance for you to make some money, Bobby. It's a chance for you to make up for a great deal of hurt and pain you caused me.
— Yeah, well, hurt and pain are occupational hazards.
— Of what, being involved with you?
— No, of being alive. Now, what the fuck did you bring me here to tell me?
She rocked back from the force of the words,
— It's about what's in Carla's wallet.
— What about it?
— It isn't a ring.

22.

Once Angie had copped to her lie about the ring, she couldn't get out of that gallery fast enough, though she did stop to Euro-kiss a couple of baldheads with fancy eyeglasses. We made our way to a parking structure halfway down Cannon; I'd parked my little toy car on four, but she hits the button for six, which strikes me as strange since she got there before me. This observation gives me a little rush of detectiveness, and I feel like my game is improving. The doors open, and we get out, her heels clicking loud off the concrete walls. She pulls out a set of keys from her bag, and double taps the alarm on what looks a like a brand new Audi.

— What happened to the Prius?

— I decided to send a thousand dollar check to Greenpeace and get myself a proper fucking car.

We get in. The car smells like a leather glove.

— When'd you get this?

— Are you really interested?

— No.

— I didn't think so.

She reaches behind the passenger seat, yanks a fancy book bag into her lap, and pulls out an old-school manila envelope with a red string clasp.

— I'm sorry I lied to you Bobby. It seemed all you needed to know was who you were looking for and what and not what it led to … I'm sure that sounds a bit cold-blooded but it made sense in my head at the time.

She unwound the string, lifted the flap on the envelope, pulled out an 8 x 10 photograph, and handed it to me. It was a picture of Carla and a man I didn't know. She was staring into the lens with a look that made the hairs stand up on the back of my neck. Sheathed in some kind of gleaming gold shirt, her mouth was curled in an untouchable smile. As for the man, he seemed about sixty with a large shaved head, dark eyes and a lantern jaw. He stood behind her, encircling her with his arms, his moonlike head resting on her gold shoulder. The photo pulsated with dark energy, and as I studied it closer I realized I was looking at the two highest people I had ever seen; her on dope, and him on her.

— Who's the guy?

— His name is Otto Schlein.

My face did something I didn't mean it to, but didn't give away that I'd heard the name before.

— He seems pretty fond of her.

She bit down on her lip, as she stared at the photo.

— You don't have any idea do you?

— About what?

— Who designed the smock?

I didn't, and I didn't care, still lost in the pull of Carla's eyes.

— Come now, take good look, I'll give you a hint. He's legendary.

I focused on the shirt. It had a tunic collar and dark hand-sewn ornamental designs on it, like planets or crowns.

— Ummmm ... Merlin the Magician?

That gave her a chuckle.

— Close ...

— Alistair Crowley.

— God no.

The way she said that gave me a chuckle.

— Just tell me.

She took a pause.

— Matisse.

— Matisse?

She nodded.

— Like *Matisse*, Matisse?

— He designed it for "Les Ballets Russes," the Russian ballet section of the Stravinsky opera *Song of the Nightingale*. It was directed by Diaghilev. Otto bought it for Carla to try and win her back.

So, Liam had been right about an "apology gift," just wrong about what it was. Things were getting more interesting by the moment.

— It hasn't turned up with her things.

— Maybe she sold it.

— No. If she sold it, I'd know. The art world isn't as big as you think. I've talked to her last lover, and the only things she left at his place were some clothes, but I know she had taken a storage locker for what she called her "personal items"—diaries, photos, an old Triumph motorcycle that belonged to her dad. She kept the key to it in her wallet. We don't know the exact number, but we know the location.

— Why don't you just talk to the storage guy and tell him the truth?

— We tried, but she gave him very clear instructions to never let anyone in but her. She paid three years in advance. Our best hope is that your friend Kyle still has the wallet.

— How much is it worth?

— The smock?

I nodded.

— A great deal, but it's not just the money, it's the provenance. Matisse, Stravinsky, and Diaghilev, all connected to the same piece.

She went back into the book bag, but this time instead of a manila envelope, she came out with a wad of cash big as Lebron James' fist.

— This is ninety-five hundred dollars. With the five hundred I already gave you that makes ten thousand.

I look at the fat loaf of cash. Now what do I fucking do? Trust a woman I don't know well, but at least have a history of sex and emotional turmoil with, or her crazy half-sister's crazy half-brother, who I've only met twice, but somehow have also seen unclothed? The obvious move is to take Angie's loot and give Liam back his five grand, but then I think to myself, why not just keep it all? Sure, I'd be betraying them both, but they're already betraying each other, and not only that, they're each looking for different things. If I find the bag and the bag has the wallet and the wallet has the key that leads to the Hockneys, then I go to Scotland. If I find the bag and the bag has the wallet and the wallet has the key that leads to Matisse, I'll go see Ange. The only thing missing is an Irishman offering me twenty grand to find the wallet, throw it in the river and forget the whole fucking thing.

Angie meets my eyes and gives me a look like, *we agree on everything, and always have,* then she hands me the wad. I put it in my inside jacket pocket. The weight of it feels good.

— Can I ask you something?

— What, sweetie?

— Do you really want me to go to Italy with you, or did you just tell me that because you want me to find the smock?

She gave it some thought.

— Both.

— Good answer.

I stroke my beard and look back down at Carla in gold.

— Mind if I hold onto the photo?
It was a request any good detective would make.

23.

There out on the sidewalk, sucking down menthols and waiting for the end of the world. I'm outside the Hollywood NA meeting on New Hampshire where I'm supposed to meet Andrew Wood, and of course, he has yet to show. Maybe he's caught in traffic after a late meeting at Disney, or maybe he's crawling around his office with enough Ketamine in his system to put Secretariat into a coma.

I had been eating a cheap, steam-table lunch of lentils and goat curry at my go-to Bangladeshi joint on Third when Wood had called sounding a bit out of sorts.

— Hello.

— Who is this?

— What?

— Who is this?

— What do you mean "who is this?" You called me.

— I know I called you ... Gotterman?

— It's Zorn, dude.

— Oh good, you're who I meant to call.

I didn't need to see a toxicology report to know there was a lot going on.

— You okay? You sound a little scattered.

— I just got into a huge argument with the parking lady at the Grove. Did you know they're all Ethiopian?

— I did.

— She wanted to charge me for a lost ticket even though I had all these bags full of books and cheese. It would have made a great movie.

— What would have?

— The argument. The two cultures not understanding each other, the lost ticket setting off a chain reaction of events that leads to some other kind of loss, bigger, global, and the subtext of the narrative: how tribal everything is.

— Sounds more like a scene than an entire movie.

— Right; the scene is just a scene, but the movie is a whole movie. Hold on, I got a call coming in, got to take this.

I heard two clicks then— "Hey Doctor Harklin, I know you hate it when I call you on your cell, but my girlfriend's Portuguese

Water Dog got run over last night and she's freaking out and I was wondering if you could prescribe her a few Xanax over the phone or if she needs to come into the office?"
— It's still me.
— Hello?
— It's still me, it's still Zorn.
— Shit, how did I drop that call? Dude, I need to go to a meeting, this is starting to not be fun.
— You want to meet me tonight at the men's stag on Masselin?
— No, I can't do AA, too much industry. I can't have people knowing I relapsed.
— OK, but when you don't show up for work 'cause you're dead, they're probably going to figure it out.
— Yeah, but at least I won't have to tell Ray I need to go to rehab.
— Do you need to go to rehab?
— Probably, but let's start with a meeting. I'll go to rehab after DreamWorks buys the pitch.

#

I'm in the back, trying to scan the crowd for Wood just in case he came early, but all I see are the enlisted men and women of a ragtag Cholo army. A brown mountain of a Mex makes his way through the crowd, handing out noisemakers from a cardboard box. His head is tapered like a soft-serve ice cream cone, and he has the facial hair of a goat. They don't call this meeting "Monday Night Madness" for nothing.

Narcotics Anonymous was started in 1953 back when dope fiends were *persona non grata*, and your standard midtown Scotch drinker didn't want to be rubbin' elbows with an uptown gutter hype no matter if he knew the third-step prayer or not. These days, what separates the two programs now is not so much the substances consumed but the station of the people consuming them. To break it down as simply as possible: AA went to college, NA went to prison.

#

The speaker is mid-share, and he makes it clear early that he doesn't give a fuck what you think, which means he probably cares a lot. His name's Charles, and I know that because the first thing he said was:

— I'm Charles, and I'm an addict. My clean date is September 27, 1994, my home group is House of Uhuru. Monday night at 7:30, I got a sponsor, and he got a sponsor, I also got me a bunch of sponsees, and man, they talk a lot of shit.

Old Charles has come all the way up from Watts to tell us how it goes, and it goes like this:

— I don't pick up no matter what *he* do, I don't pick up no matter what *she* do, I don't pick up no matter what my *momma* do, I don't pick up no matter what the *dog* do, I just don't pick up. And I don't play gangster either, 'cause I been to prison and they ain't got nothing there for me. If that's your get-down, cool, but that ain't my get-down. I ain't sayin' you bad, 'cause God don't make bad people. I just sayin' you gonna have to get yo ass up and the hell away from me.

And he busts a laugh just for punctuation, and the room is hanging on every word and givin' it back with calls of "that's right" and "preach brother," and one big, blonde Latina with her hair tied high like Pebbles Flintstone, stamps her foot and yips, "that's real talk" and Charles steps back from the mic, and lets it all just simmer in the moonlight. And once he's wrung every drop he can out of that beat, he baby-steps forward, cranes out his neck like he's coming in for a kiss.

— People say 12-step is brainwashin'. Well let me tell y'all something, after all the shit I got up to, I *needed* my brain washed.

And he adds a "huh," like a rim shot, and the crowd eats that up too. I'm still near the back, sandwiched between a demonic frat boy in plaid shorts, and a dark, Persian girl with black jeans, black jacket, black hair, black eyes, and a black mustache worthy of the baritone in a barbershop quartet. She smells like wet leather and cumin, and though it's a tad mildewed, I just can't help but grab another whiff.

I feel a buzz in my pocket. I don't want to be disrespectful to all the crackheads, so I step outside before I give it a glimpse. It's a text from Wood: "Note session with writer went long, let's try again tomorrow."

My first thought isn't, *oh no, Wood's out there getting high*, it's: *what writer is he giving notes to, is he getting paid, and if so, why isn't it me?*

I slip the phone back in my pocket and catch a nod from a frail, old brother just walking in. He's wearing a maroon, Goodwill three-piece, and rocks a "conk" he's probably had since doo-wop night at the Shrine Auditorium. I'm tempted to drag him to a corner and find out where he copped and who from, but before I can make a move I feel a hot wind burning my ear.

— What are you doing here, slummin'?

I turn to the voice and find two dark eyes smirking at me.

— What's going on, Lupita? Long time no see.

— Hear you're looking for Kyle.

— Who told you that?

— About ten different people.

— Really? I barely know ten people.

I looked her up and down. She put a little hip into it.

— You been in touch with him?

— Maybe.

— You know where he is?

— Maaaybeee.

She flashed her eyes and skipped away up the concrete ramp.

— Where you going?

— That's for you to find out.

24.

We hadn't gone three blocks, and she was already camped out in the shotgun seat like we'd been running partners for years. I tried to steer the focus toward Kyle, but she was more interested in Carla.

— I'm not saying it was her karma, but she must have done something bad, 'cause it's hard to OD with a habit like that unless you're reckless as hell.

— You OD'd a bunch of times with a habit like that.

— Yeah, and I was reckless as hell.

She took a drag off her smoke. I could hear the lipstick.

— He was just copping for her at first, that's all it was, he was just gettin' her issue, making a little something for himself. I was over there a few times when she called.

— Over where?

— Hollywood, he had a studio on Serrano or maybe it was a bachelor. I never know the difference.

— A bachelor doesn't have a kitchen.

— Then it was a studio, but he wasn't cooking a lot of meals.

— I'll bet. I'm sure eating in general was on the back burner.

— Yeah, you're the only fat junkie I ever knew.

There were other fat junkies, but since I wasn't fat no more I let it slide.

— He didn't want me meeting her, so he'd go down and wait for her in front and I'd watch out the window. She'd come down from the hills in her Mercedes. She was living with some rich Hollywood fuck who was trying to keep her clean. Had one of those sober companions chasing after her she was always trying to ditch. When she'd finally get loose she'd call all urgent, and be like "Kyle, I need your help *now*." She never said, "Do you have anything?" or "What's going on?" She always said "I need your help." She had the poor little rich girl thing down pat.

I looked over and caught the half-lit shadow of a dark-haired head in motion, the white filter of a half-smoked Kent between chipped red nails.

— He's not gonna wanna see you, trust me. And not because of our shit.

She brought the smoke to her mouth, and settled in profile, the Filipina in her catching the light with a shine.

— I never told him. And I know *you* didn't.

She blew her smoke out the window, and when she came back around I saw she'd lost a tooth on top.

— He doesn't need to know about all that. It was a one-off anyway. Not even a one-off. Besides, makes me look bad, not you. You're just a dude, the world forgives a dude, he just can't forgive himself. A woman can't forgive herself, but the world won't forgive her either.

— Where'd you hear that?

— Radio Lupita.

She turned with a smile like she'd gotten off a good one.

— You still reading Bukowski?

— Nah, that was just a phase. I mean, I still love him, I'll always love him, but he's a young girl's writer.

— He gets you to turn the page, I'll give him that.

— Yeah, you said that to me once before.

— Well, it must be a good line if I'm using it twice.

When I first met Kyle, Lupita had a few months clean and was taking English classes at Santa Monica College. The three of us used to grab coffee, and me and her would chop it up about books and writers. Then she relapsed, and we chopped it up about her staying away from Kyle.

— I'm kind of obsessed with *The Master and Margarita* at the moment. You know it?

— Yeah, Bulgakov right? I never read it, but I know it's a book women like. A lot of *Master and Margarita* fans on OkCupid.

She put her foot on the dashboard and her dress fell away at the knee, her legs weren't missing any teeth, that's for damn sure.

— You still writing poetry?

— Just to pay the bills.

— Any new scripts?

— No, but I'm recording everything we say, so I may have one before the night's over.

— I wouldn't put it past you.

— Come on, I wouldn't do that. Besides, anything really good, I'll remember.

She flicked her smoke out the window.

— Damn son, you clean a long time, that career shit shoulda come back already.

She had switched from literary critic back to Boyle Heights Chola.

— I know, if I ever get another agent that's exactly what I'm going to tell them.

She rolled her eyes and gave me a little chuckle. She may have been beat to shit, but she was still a beautiful brown girl, and the teeth that were left were perfect, and white as dice.

— Turn here.

— Where we going?

— You want me to take you to Kyle or not?

I took a left on 8th Street. The part that can't figure out if it's Korea or Guadalajara.

— Don't worry, sir. You're in good hands.

The way she said "sir" bounced off the windshield and punched me in the throat.

— I'm mad at you, you know. I really am.

— Oh yeah.

— It was as much him as it was me.

— I'm sure it was. I'm sure it was both of you and neither of you.

— What does that mean?

— It means you're both addicts, you get addicted to things, it's not your fault, but when you get addicted to a person and the person you're addicted to is also addicted to the drug you're addicted to, it's probably not going to work out.

— It wasn't just an addiction. It was love too.

— Yeah. You were in love with each other's lunacy.

— What do you know about it?

— I know you used to call me going "I got to get away from Kyle, he's sapping my blood," And I wasn't even your sponsor. You should have heard the calls I got from *him*.

— That's why what you did was so fucked up.

— What *I* did? What are you, a Catholic schoolgirl?

— You wish.

— It was fucked up, okay? I feel awful about it. You know that. I told you how sorry I was.

— Damn boy, calm down, it wasn't that fucked up. Nobody got killed. It was just. It was just a lot. You understand things about me, you know, you just cut right through everything and got to it. You're very perceptive, sir.

— Yeah, a lot of good it's done me.

We stopped at the light at Catalina. There's a liquor store there that has one of those old-school neon signs that makes drinking seem like a great American art form. The red glow from it was mixed up in Lupita's hair, which was cut in a jet-black bob long enough to cover the tracks on her neck. She was wearing a vintage blue dress with a Peter Pan collar, and a pair of low, maroon Doc Martins with the yellow stitching like it was 1985. On a white girl they'd have been cliché and dated, on a half-Filipina dope fiend they were ironic and beyond reproach.

— I need you to take me somewhere.

— What kind of somewhere?

— It'll be quick.

— You're not clean?

Her silence answered that one.

— What were you doing at the meeting?

— I don't know, just somewhere to go between shots.

It was a good line, and I was thinking about relapsing, just so I could use it.

— You really think I'm going to take you to cop right now?

— I don't know, sir, depends on how bad you want to find Kyle.

#

— Come in with me.

— Come on, Lupita, give me a break.

— You're gonna make me go in there alone?

— What would you do if I wasn't here?

— I'd go in there alone, and I have to deal with a whole thing.

— What whole thing?

— What do you think?

— That's your hustle now?

— Fuck you. The day I start fucking for drugs is the day you can put a bullet in my head. Now, money's another story.

— *That's* your hustle?

— I'm just kidding, sir.

She gave me a pigeon-toed, little-girl look that made me think she might not be kidding.

— Look, you want cop, do your thing, but I'm going to pass on the chaperone role.

— Please.

— Lupita.

— Please, I need to get straight in there, the bathroom doesn't have a lock and I won't feel safe without someone watching.

— You're about to score and fix in a dope house every cop in L.A. knows, I think the safety issue's pretty much out the window.

— It's not a dope house.

— Come on, man, I know this spot.

— It's not that spot anymore. And don't call me man. I hate that.

— Okay. So, it's a new spot, same building.

— It's not the same building, it's the one next door.

We were on 23rd just east of Vermont, a few blocks below the freeway. We were parked in front of one of those big old craftsmen that's been broken into four apartments. The one on the far right was the old dope house, which was 24-7; knock on the door, if they were there they were there, if they weren't they weren't. The main guy was a young Central American kid name Jaime who smoked coke, sold junk, and let people fix on the couch, a truly hellish combination.

— Is it still Jaime?

— No, he's dead.

She looked at me, her eyes going milk chocolate from bittersweet.

— Please, kind sir, I'd be most appreciative if you would escort me.

— Jesus Christ, you're a fucking terrorist, you know that.

— Please, daddy.

— That's not going to work.

— Daddy, daddy, daddy, daddy, *daddy*.

— Stop.

— Dude, I need to get right, just come in there and watch my back, you know what it's like to be a girl down here.

— Yeah, it's easier.

— Not for a brown girl.

— Lupita.

— Just come with me, I'll help you find Kyle, I promise.

— You got a spot or you going to be in there for an hour?

I was asking if she had a dependable vein or whether she was going to poke away and hope for the best.

— I have something in my shoulder, I'll muscle it if I have to.

— No, you won't.

— I will, I promise. Beside I can always put it in the vein near my kitty.

I flashed on the image of her sitting on a toilet with her brown legs parted and a needle in her inner thigh but couldn't decide whether it was appalling or exciting.

— You really know where Kyle is?

— I can help you find him.

— You can help me find him or you know where he is?

— Which will make you come in with me?

#

A big off-brand flat-screen plays Mexican soccer on mute. Lupita's over in the corner, bartering with a young 18th Street type named Flaco, the prerequisite teardrop tattoo falling from his eye. As for me, I'm standing near the door playing the part of the nervous white guy, my least favorite role in the world. Flaco's keeping one eye on me, as Lupita spits her desperation in his ear. I glance over to the couch where some soot-colored brother sits in a trance, a crack stem in one hand and a lime green Bic lighter in the other.

— Moth to flame, moth to flame, moth to flame, moth to flame.

That's his mantra, and he's sticking with it. Flaco spins away from Lupita's ear and heads toward me.

— She's twenty short.

— What do you want me to do about it?

He looks at me like I'm a long way from home.

— I don't know, bra, but somebody gonna have to come up with the twenty dollars.

— I'm sure she's good for it.

— She say you got her.

I looked over his shoulder at Lupita.

— What's going on?

— You ain't gotta talk to her, just talk to me.

He gives me a dose of his big eyes, the kind that only belong to saints and killers.

— I'm not sure what you want me to say.

— Don't say shit.

So, I don't, but that doesn't make him happy either.

— Look here, your girl's twenty light. You gonna put it straight?

— Moth to flame, moth to flame, moth to flame.

— She say you got her. You got her or not?

And the cat on the couch brings the moth to the flame, and I hear the dry gurgle of crack cocaine being sucked through hot steel wool. When he lets out the cloud, the wet stink nearly buckles my knees.

— Yeah, I got her.

I reach in my pocket, peel off a twenty and hand it to him.

— This bitch just played you, fool.

#

— Are you kidding me?

— What?

— What the fuck was that? If you were short, why didn't you just tell me in the car?

— I wasn't short. He just got stupid with me.

We're headed for the bathroom at the end of the hallway, walking on a foul running carpet with a plastic runner over it so you don't get filth on the filth.

— What were you whispering to him?

— Nothing, just nonsense.

— What kind of nonsense?

— The kind you whisper to little Salvadorian boys to get them do what you want.

We pass the brown, rectangular stain of a pay phone that's been ripped out of the wall. It's like a cave panting from a lost culture. Lupita pushes a door open and I'm hit with a heady mix of piss and Ajax.

— Coming in?

— I thought you wanted me to watch the door?

— Yeah, from inside.

— How am I going to watch it from inside?

— It's got a little slidey lock. If someone tries to come in, we'll hear 'em.

— I thought there wasn't a lock.

— There isn't, not one that'll do anything. Just come in.

I bring my voice even lower than it already is and whisper,

— I don't want to watch you fix.

She makes her voice louder and barks:

— Will you stop being a little bitch!

I follow her inside. She flips the tiny dead bolt and gets to work. Out from her bag comes a half-full ten-pack of syringes, a pair of hemostats (the kind hip folks used to use for a roach clip) and a small, blackened cooker like they hand out with bleach and cotton at the "needle exchange." She spits a small green balloon out of her mouth that looks a dime but might be a twenty and bites it open. The dope's in the cooker and the cooker's got heat on it before I even get a chance to think "what the fuck am I doing here?" The junk bubbles brown, giving off its vinegar stink, but this time instead of puking in my mouth, I get a warm tingle behind my ears. She lays the cooker on the sink, removes a tiny blue-tinted ziplock from her bra strap, and tips a little coke in like she's tapping the ash off a cigarette.

— You're doing a speedball?

— That's far from a speedball, sir.

She drops a piece of cotton in the cooker and it puffs up brown. She pulls a rig out of the pack, takes off the orange safety cap, and holds it in her mouth. I might as well be watching porn.

— I hate Termuros.

I'm referring to the brand of syringe. She takes the rig out of her mouth.

— Beggars can't be choosers and they're called Terumos, though your dyslexia is very charming.

Lupita draws up the shot, pulling the wet brown cotton dry. She flicks the syringe, gets rid of the air, holds up the rig, and admires her handiwork. Then she pushes the outfit toward me.

— Okay.

— Okay what?

— Okay, I need you to hit me.

25.

— I just wanna be good, you know. That's all I want, just that. I don't care if I ever have a kid or leave my mark or any of that, I just want to clean up, and be good and get a job, and have a little house with a tree, and pay my car insurance, and just a live a life. Just be good.

She takes a drag off her Kent and lets the smoke fall out of her mouth.

— I been bad so long I should just wear a big scarlet "B" on my chest.

— You're not bad.

— Yes, I am. I'm scurrilous.

When she had pushed the rig at me in the bathroom, I pushed it right back, but she pouted so good I agreed to give it a shot. Pun intended.

I put the rig in my mouth like a dog bone and examined the inside of her thin brown arm. It was scarred and scuffed from shoulder to wrist. I picked a spot, and set a three-poke limit, the fist jab going into her bicep, and failing miserably. My second attempt was in the vein that bridged the top of her hand with back of her wrist. I was more surprised than she was when the hot, black blood gushed in. She gasped and met my eyes as I pushed it in slow.

— Scurrilous, huh?

— Well, maybe not scurrilous, but I haven't been doing my best.

We were tucked by a dumpster in the parking lot of the Brite Spot Diner in Echo Park. Lupita stashed her smoke between her lips and took off her Doc Martens. She shifted around so her back was against the door, and straightened her legs putting her little, white socks in my lap.

— Well, here we are, sir. Reunited at last.

The line wasn't delivered as well as a few of her others, but that didn't stop me from taking her foot.

— Why you looking for Kyle?

— You tell me, you seem to know everything.

— I just heard you were looking for him. I rubbed her foot softly, but hard enough to see a bit of her teeth.

— You gonna spoil me.

— I already spoiled you.

She smiled out of her half-shut eyes.

— You shot me up good, sir.

— Yeah, let's try and keep that between you and me.

She made a tick-a-lock gesture and I pushed my thumb a little harder into the soft curve of her arch. She rolled her eyes back like she had everything she could ever need, and let the smoke roll up into the little black holes in her nose.

— You gonna tell me why you're looking for him?

— Just got to do with Carla. And whatever went wrong down at the Snooty.

— That's funny.

— What is?

— When brown junkies die in a crack motel they just get dead, but when some fancy white bitch dies something "went wrong."

She pulled her feet out of my hands and spun around so she was facing forward.

— Time for me to go home.

— What?

She began to put her shoes back on.

— What's wrong?

— Nothing's wrong, show's over. I'll give you back your twenty next time I see you.

— I thought you were going to help me find Kyle.

— Changed my mind.

— Now that I drove you to cop and shot you up.

— Take me home.

— What happened? Is this because I said something "went wrong?"

— What was he supposed to do, call 911 and wait for the cops? There was nothing he could do; the bitch was dead.

— How do you know?

— Because I saw him right after. He was in front of my place, when I got home. Had some of her shit with him.

— What shit?

— Just some of her shit.

— Was there a gold shirt?

— What?

I reached behind me, grabbed the manila envelope off the back seat, and took out the picture of Carla and Otto.

— That gold shirt. Did he have it?

She studied the picture.

— No.

— Tell me the fucking truth.

— I am.

— He didn't have a gold shirt?

— No.

— Do you?

— No.

— Lupita, please, if you know anything about this you have to tell me.

— I don't have her shirt. Fuck. The only thing I have of hers is this.

She dug down between her feet and came up with a black bag, the one she'd had with her the whole night.

— That's Carla's?

She gave me a scared nod.

— Was there a wallet in it?

She reached in and pulled out a tan leather wallet.

— This?

— Give me that.

— What's going on?

I grabbed the wallet out of her hands, spread it open and felt for the key. It wasn't in the billfold or the change purse. I dug into every corner, and felt along every seam, but there was no key.

— Let me see the bag.

She paused, and I pulled the bag away from her and tore into it, looking for little pockets, or stash places. There was nothing but girl shit.

— Did you look through the wallet when you got it?

— Of course.

— You didn't find a key?

— A house key?

— Any key.

— No.

— Did Kyle mention anything about a storage space?

— No, what's going on, is Kyle in trouble?

— Where's Kyle? Do you have a number for him, a number that works?

— Yeah, but I want to know what's going on.

— Give me your phone.

— No.

— Call him, when you get him just put me on.

— No. Who's that baldhead dude?

I lunged for the glove compartment and she jumped back like I was going to hit her. I reached in and came out with the thick roll Angie laid on me.

— Get him on the phone, I'll give you a hundred bucks.

— Where did you get that?

— Get him.

— Okay, but for five not one.

— Fuck no. I'll give you two.

— Five.

— Look, just call him and if he answers I'll give you three hundred.

— I'm not going to be getting him in trouble, am I?

— No.

She dug through Carla's bag and pulled out her phone.

— I knew nothing good could come from him hooking up with that bitch.

She scrolled for Kyle's number, then tapped. I watched her listening to it ring.

— Yo, it's me, you straight? Yeah, me too.

She was talking to him, but her eyes were on me.

— I know, shit gets crazy out there. Hey, I'm here with someone who wants to talk to you, I'm gonna put him on.

She handed me the phone.

— What's up Colonel?

I'd figure I'd play it loose and cool like we had just talked last week.

— Who's this?

— What do you mean, who's this? It's young Bob.

Nothing.

— It's Zorn, dude.

— Oh, hey. Haven't heard from you in awhile.

— I could say the same of you. It's good to hear your voice.

— You too.

He didn't mean it.

— What are you doing with Lupita?

— Bumped into her at a 12-step gathering.

— Yeah, I try to stay away from those.

— Me too, but sometimes I forget myself and get sucked back in. So, where you at, I want to talk you about something.

— I know. Robert Lee told me you were asking Captain all kinds of questions. I'm trying to put that shit behind me, dude.

— Yeah, how's that working for you?

It was the kind of thing a sponsor says and I could feel him bristle.

— They think I just left her there?

— No.

— What do they think?

— What does who think?

— Her sister, dude. I know she's been trying to find me, and I know you like dated her or did some fucked-up shit to her or something.

— I didn't do any fucked-up shit to her. Let's just get together tomorrow, I'll tell you everything I know.

Silence.

— Kyle, look, I got no fucking judgment on this shit and I'm sure whatever happened is plenty fucked up as it is, but now somehow, I'm involved, and what you know might really help me and what I know might really help you.

— There was nothing I could do.

— I believe you. Let's just get together tomorrow.

Nothing.

— Just text me tomorrow.

Nothing.

— Kyle?

— OK, I'll text you.

— Great. And be careful tonight, just do a bunch of little shots and don't be a maniac with the coke.

— Don't worry, I know how to shoot drugs.

— That's what I'm afraid of.

I was hoping for at least a chuckle, but he was gone.

— What the fuck, dude? What's going on, what did he do, who's that bitch's sister?

I looked down at the phone and quickly tried to remember Kyle's number.

— What are you doing? I'll give you his fucking number. Give me my phone back and give me my three hundred dollars. Damn boy, what's wrong with you, you ain't slick.

I gave her back the phone and peeled off three C-notes like

having a big dick wad of dough was my natural state.
— Here, but just answer my calls or texts, OK?
— I'm not making any promises.
— Fine, then just take $200.
— Just give me the three. You know I'd answer you if you didn't give me a dime. I happen to like talking to you, sir.
It was a $100 dollar "sir"; I handed her the dough.
— But seriously man, what did he do?
— He got mixed up with a fancy junkie.
I pulled the cigarette out of her mouth and took a drag.

26.

Canter's Deli is open twenty-four hours every day of the year except Yom Kippur, and if you need some mediocre pastrami at 3 a.m., it's the place to go. If it's before two, you can go to Greenblatt's on Sunset, but that's a whole other situation. They shave it thin and it's halfway to the gentile pastrami they sell at every drive-thru in L.A., most famously Johnnie's on Sepulveda where the meat is so salty you need a bag of IV fluids after half a sandwich.

I'm at Canter's, camped out at the counter in the back, staring at the big slabs of watermelon they keep in an old chrome refrigerated case. I'm working on a meal of pickles, chopped liver, raw onion, and egg salad I'm smearing on buttered rye. I was hoping a little Jew food might soothe my soul, but five bites in I'm regretting the decision deeply. As a wise, old AA veteran once told me, "You have a really bad idea of what will make you feel good."

I wipe the schmaltz off my hands, reach for the envelope with the red string, and get a little private time with Carla.

#

I can't stop looking at her freckles. Weightless and innocent, they remind me that it is often the most tender souls who go down in the most lurid tales. She looks *much* higher here than she did the day we met, her eyes glazed and glowing like a smacked-back leopard. What the hell did those eyes see in Kyle? He was a take-the-bus junkie, and all his charm was in who he *didn't* know, not who he did, though one should never be surprised by what a man and woman can agree upon when no one else is looking. Maybe after all the fancy assholes who'd tried to shoot, mount, and stuff her, Kyle was just what she needed. She had a taxidermy gleam in this picture, that's for sure.

The waitress, a gray skinned woman who's spent way too much time under fluorescent lights, rips a check off her pad and puts it down in front of me. She points toward the yellow and brown mush on my plate.

— You taking that with you?

— That's okay; I want to live through the week.

She doesn't even crack a smile, and that's when I hear:
— Bobby Zorn.
I spin around to find some good-looking tall dude with an even better-looking girl. He's wearing a pale blue James Dean windbreaker, khaki pants and black Jack Purcells. I have absolutely no idea who he is.
— It's Dennis. Dennis Destitrino.
Great, the executive from DreamWorks spots me at Canter's and I draw a blank.
— Oh, hey dude. I didn't recognize you looking so casual.
He pulls out the appropriate smile and relieves me of all embarrassment. It's a pro move.
— This is Canada.
He indicates the girl, a leggy brunette in a black blazer who can go either softcore porn or CNN anchorwoman. I give her my best "I'm a wise old battered mystic grin, she hits me back with a wall of inhumanly perfect teeth.
— So, what are you guys doing in this fine Semitic establishment at this late hour?
— We were over at the Troubadour.
— Oh yeah, were the Doors playing?
That got a chuckle out of him even though the Doors are more famous for playing "The Whiskey."
— I had to go see Neon Trees. We might use one of their songs in *My Sister Is a Witch 2*.
I had heard of neither Neon Trees or *My Sister Is a Witch 1*, but nodded anyway like I was right with him.
— I was in with Jeffrey yesterday and I gave him the one line on the jukebox thing. His ears perked up.
— Cool. I'm looking forward to telling him about it.
— He didn't really seem to remember who you were when I mentioned your name, but I'm sure he will when he sees your face.
It caught me flush on the jaw, and I could feel my knees buckle.
— As soon as there's an opening in his schedule, I'll let Oren know.
— Great. Can't wait.
If he has a smile for this situation he doesn't use it, and off they go on four long legs, back to wherever lean and fortunate people hole up for the evening. When I come back around, my waitress is knocking my food into a white Styrofoam box.
— You said you want it or you don't?

Who the fuck cares about chopped liver? Jeffrey Katzenberg doesn't know who I am.

#

I park my little toy car in my little toy parking spot and stumble through the narrow hedge-lined path to the front. It's late and I've been up since the Bible was written. A lot of shit happened today, though a lot of shit always happens, even if it's just in my head.

I stop at the mailbox, hoping it's full of good not bad, though having ten Gs in my pocket sure takes some of the drama out of it. I squeeze my paw in the narrow slot, and wonder what was skinnier back in the '30s, the hands or the mail? I come out with a deck of white envelopes including the car bill, the cable bill and the gas bill. I don't have immediate plans to pay any of them, but it's nice to know I could if I wanted to.

The last envelopes are a monthly Scientology alert for a guy named Adam Baracera, a subscription beg from *The American Poetry Review*, and a missive from one Sonya Kapp, a woman I met years ago on a sordid chat site and who lives in the wild brambles of New Brunswick, Canada. She also happens to write a damn fine letter, and I can't resist sneaking a peak at the opening paragraph, as I walk up the stairs to my pad.

"Thanks for asking about the smelts, but it's still too cold for 'em. They run when the maple leaves are as big as a moose's ear. It's just cold enough to ice fish for white perch, though. I caught about a dozen before my nostrils started freezing shut the other day. The blueberry barrens lie frozen as well but God almighty, they're beautiful no matter the season. I'm in pain and a little shack whacky as I haven't left the house, but at least once an hour I wonder what you're doing."

It's a long letter but just that first run has me feeling a familiar combination of good and bad. It's also kept me from noticing that some young, hard white dude with a tight beard and pompadour is waiting at the top of my stairs and he doesn't look happy to see me. He lets me climb all the way up before he asks:

— Are you Robert Zorn?

I barely get the "yeah" out before he throws the first punch.

27.

It lands on my temple and I get a gush of terror like an air bag just inflated in my brain. I duck and cover my head and he lets go with another huge shot that hits me in the ribs like a tire iron. I have absolutely no idea what to do, I've never been in a fight before, and the whole thing seems insane to me. Now he drives down with a fist on the top of my head and I realize—I'm fucking pissed. I grunt, get low and launch myself into him with my big Polish hips, smashing him hard against the mailbox on the wall.

I assume the fact that I have equaled his aggression with my own means the fight is over and now we are going to talk, but he has a different assumption, and kicks me in the stomach with a scream, and now he's on me, and I can't get my footing and I'm scared he's going to throw me down the steps. I claw for the railing yelling "Stop, stop!" but he won't, and lands a boxer's punch to my face that echoes like a gun shot, and I go down for real, face flat on the concrete floor. He stands over me and I hear the breath firing from his nose like a horse in the dead of winter. I'm waiting for him to shove a gun in my mouth and say, "Leave the detective work to the professionals, asshole!" or "The art belongs to Otto!"

— Stay away from Zamine, motherfucker!

I choke out the words "I don't know any Zamine."

But this just makes him angrier and he stomps at my chest with the heel of his boot.

— The girl from the bank, asshole!

He reaches into his pocket, pulls out a white piece of paper and shoves it in my face.

— THE GIRL FROM THE BANK!

On the paper is a Xerox copy of one of my returned checks. He points at it and hisses.

— I know where you live, asshole, I know where you fucking live!

And then for good Armenian measure, he spits on me before kicking me out of the way and heading down the stairs.

28.

The wind is drunk and disorderly and the streetlights are swaying like church bells on Sunday morning. Last night it was downright riotous and now everywhere you look dead, brown palm fronds are scattered like the fossilized wings of extinct pterodactyls. Add that to the trash blowing knee-high through the gutters, and the entire city feels post-apocalyptic. If I saw two guys jump out of a car, smash a man over the head with a brick and steal his pants I'd chalk it up to the breeze. And that's how it goes out here. The wind is famous for making you nuts. "The Santa Anas will make you crazy." That's what I've been hearing since I first got here.

I'm driving south on Wilton, through the tropic of Pupusa, and down into craftsman alley. This is my jugular vein for mid-city travel, a carotid artery that splits this town in half and gets me where I need to go, which is usually nowhere. I pull the rearview down and take a peek at myself. Which I've been doing every thirty seconds since I got in the car. My jaw isn't as swollen as it should be but I'm wearing a nice purple and blue shiner around my left eye. It's a nasty little piece of business, but for some reason it's got me feeling kinda jaunty, like I wanna mouth off for no good reason.

After Grygor (the name I assigned Zamine's boyfriend) left me battered and spat-on, I crawled into the house, and with no ice on hand, held a frozen loaf of Orowheat potato bread to my face. That's what's kept the jaw swelling down, but the black eye caught me by surprise. It gives me a certain Private Dick gravitas, but if anyone asks how I got it, I don't think I'll be telling them it was proper comeuppance for being a dirty old man.

I take the little curve on 1st and wait at the three-way light. I've driven this particular stretch so many times I know each house personally: the light blue with the three gabled roof and the brown trim, the beige with the glass-enclosed porch and the oak door wide enough for an elephant, the brown and green with the rafter tails poking out under the eaves like oars on a Viking ship, and then that crazy gray number with the white Greek columns, like the builder started reading Plato halfway through and just couldn't help himself. No one walks the streets in this town, they drive, and when half your waking reality goes by between twenty-five and forty miles an hour, the homes become the people, and your neighbors aren't men and women, but architecture. Craftsman, Mid-Century, Spanish Revival, those are the nationalities of L.A., not Mexican, Korean and Armenian. The homes are the soul of this city, the people themselves are just driving through.

I touch my eye and see how hard I can push before I wince. Not very hard. I'm south on Wilton 'cause I'm headed down to Robert Lee's to meet Kyle, after waking up to this text:

"Not feeling it today, let's just do it tomorrow."

It was sent at 5:43 a.m. so either he had been shooting coke all night and the idea of having to actually interact with another human seemed implausible or he had shot all his dope, didn't have a wake-up, and was in a holding pattern until whatever his current dealer deemed a reasonable hour to do business.

I saw the text at 9:45, the latest I've slept since I got off methadone. Must have been the beat-down I took, and the dregs of bourbon a woman named Loretta left in my cabinet a few years back. I guess you could consider it a relapse, but I'm not the mood to call my sponsor and confess. Beside I don't like booze anyway. If I'm still drinking in a week, I'll call the paramedics; if I end up shooting dope, someone else probably will. When I read Kyle's text I could tell his already cold feet were getting frigid, so I decided to stop playing coy and hit him back with:

— Let's just do today. There's money involved ... Enough so you'll only be up at five in the morning if you want to be.

A minute later my phone lit up with "my day just opened up, meet me at Robert Lee's at 1." Money, sex, or drugs. Offer one of those three and you can usually get someone's attention.

I get down between 4th and 6th and it seems every other house has been converted into a Korean nursery school. I'm thinking about whether I would have pulled a gun on Grygor if I'd had one, when my phone rings. It is none other than Andrew Wood. My chance to mouth off just showed up.

— Don't tell me, you're in prison in Bangkok.

— No, just County. Can you bail me out?

— You're not serious?

— Of course not. I'm at the top of my game, dude. I have so many things to discuss with you, it's been an insane twenty-four hours.

I didn't doubt it.

— Were your ears burning 'cause I was talking about you last night? We gotta figure out what we're doing next.

— What do you mean next? We still got to pitch this Jukebox thing.

— That's a layup. You're going to own Jeffrey. I know it. I wish I could bet on it in Vegas. The question is: what are we doing after that? You're coming back strong and I want to be part of it.

All I could think was "own Jeffrey?" He doesn't even remember who I am.

— Do you know Yonah Melber?

— No, does he sell knishes?

— That's funny.

It *was* funny, but he had no idea why.

— No, he's a producer. He made a grip of money with those *Dull Knife* movies.

— The horror movies?

— Yeah, but he's done with that, he wants to win Oscars.

— Well, wish him luck for me.

— He wants to win them with you. That's who I was talking to about you. I was at the Soho House having a meeting with that Indian kid I was telling you about, who came up with the algorithm for how audiences process information.

The Soho House is a private rooftop club where the vile and talentless gather to overpay for shitty food and generally be repulsive. I've had to go there for a few meetings, and every time I leave I feel like joining ISIS.

— You never told me about an Indian kid with an algorithm.

— I did, but it doesn't matter. What matters is I ran into Yonah. He was there with his mother. I never realized how hot Israeli women are. Is your mom hot?

— My mom is old and dead and not Israeli.

— Nice. Look, Yonah's got money to develop, dude, and he's open to everything. He wants to meet with you.

— Fine, let me know when. Just not at the Soho House.

— Great, but that's not why I called. Jeffrey's office reached out. We're on for tomorrow afternoon at 4:30.

Talk about burying the lede.

— We are going to see fucking Jeffrey, dude! Now do you wanna meet later and get this shit Zoe-Saldana-tight or do you think we should just let it breathe?

— Let it breathe.

— Cool, it's breathing. Now let me ask you a different and totally theoretical question. Do you really use lemon juice to dissolve Persian heroin?

#

I'm back down below Adams, and it's becoming a regular thing. "Keep going to the barber shop and eventually you'll get a haircut." That's an old AA trope about sober dudes hanging out in bars, but I'm not hanging out in bars, I'm just shooting up Filipinas and going through the lost and found at crack motels.

When I turn into Robert Lee's driveway, he's standing in the yard swinging a golf club. By yard I mean a small patch of wheezing grass that hasn't been watered since King marched through Selma. I pull behind his little white truck and walk over, but he doesn't even look up. I used to see this guy twice a day for years, I know his sons, his wife Clara, and that she's the head of housekeeping at the Bonaventure Hotel. I know that he actually did march with King, back in the "struggle," and that when I was half dead on benzos and blood pressure medicine, it was Robert Lee who kept me from unkindness after I crashed into some Crip's Buick up the block. So, I know this cat very well, but instead of saying "Goddamn, Bobby, it's good to see you" he's just swinging his club like we saw each other yesterday.

— The secret to the fo-iron is you got to commit, you can't be half-assin' or just droppin' it on the ball like you does a pitching wedge.

He takes a swing.

— See, I pulled off that one lil' bit, didn't commit. I told you I used to caddie for Charlie Sifford, right?

— About ten times.

Finally, he turns and looks at me.

— What's goin' on, son?

Robert Lee is a big, dark, well-worn cat, streetwise and countrified at the same time. He hails from Greenwood, Mississippi and claims he used to be a pimp, but what sixty-five-year-old brother worth knowing doesn't? L.A.'s different than New York in that not a lot of black folks have been here more than a generation or two, so there's still a lot of the Delta in the way they talk, especially the older dudes. When Bob says my name he pronounces it Bow-Be.

— What happened to your eye, Bow-Be?

— Caught an elbow playin' three on three at the Y.

— Up there in Hollywood? I had an ol' pardner used to play up there. Full court.

He said "full court" to remind me I was just a white boy no matter how down I thought I was.

— You lookin' good, Robert Lee.

— You too, son, we was talkin' about you the other day. That movie 'bout the girl playin' football come on.

— Nice. How your health, holdin' up?

He took a pause and squinted up at me like the sun was shining.

— You know.

I did.

— Family good?

— They good. Clara good. Saddite think he got a tryout with the Chargers, and Kareem still fuckin' with that rap.

— How's Bob Jr.?

— He got to stop making them babies. You ain't can get Kareem a look in your business, let him drive some shit around or somethin'?

— Wish I could, I ain't rollin' like I was back then. What's with the arthritis, you hurtin'?

— Ain't too bad. But I still got the anxiety. Backed off for a minute, but now it come back hard.

Bob pronounced anxiety "angziertee" and when he got it he'd walk all night through the streets of South Central.

— Saw Captain the other day.

— Yeah, he told me.

He crinkled his nose like something smelled bad.

— He supposed to be on by with a battery for the truck, but he got his hands on some money last night so who know where he be off to.

— Why don't you ask Junior for a battery?

— Junior ain't got no battery for no truck.

He pulled a pack of smokes out of his shirt pocket and dug one out with a long black ET finger. Then ran the back of his hand under a little scrub of chin beard and lit up.

— What you doin' gettin' wrapped back up in some bullshit like this?

It was a good question and I didn't have a good answer.

— He ain't do nothin' to that girl, you know that.

— I don't think he did.

— She called me one time for somethin' and come on by herself. I thought Bob Jr. was gonna lose his mind. He said, "Damn, that girl is fine." I said you married with two kids and a pregnant wife, boy, you ain't got nothin' for that girl.

I smiled.

— She ain't need to die like that.

I didn't know if he meant young from an overdose or in a sleazy spot like the Snooty.

— You been seein' Kyle a lot?

— Was a while back, but I ain't seen him since all that went down, 'cept right after. So, you ain't drinkin' neither huh?

— I never drank.

— Well, you should have. Shit. Alcohol and weed work for you when you young.

— Well, I ain't young.

— Was when I met you.

It was the early '90s, and after Kenny had the accident Robert Lee would come and bring him his issue. After Kenny died we were left with each other.

— Kyle always late. Even when he sick he late.

He took another long drag on his Marlboro and stared out like life was nothing but a hoax.

— Y'all ain't too close no more, is you?

— That what he told you?

— He didn't have to tell me. How you gonna be close anyways, you out the game, he not.

That bad smell got back in his nose, and he slumped his shoulders.

— I be honest with you Bow-Be, I ain't happy to see you.

— Oh yeah, why's that?

— You know why. Ain't nothing 'round here for you, son. Most folks ain't get away from it all that one time, you think you gonna get away from it twice?

— Hey, I'm just looking for Kyle, Robert Lee, I'm not here for anything else.

— All right, Bow-Be, I hope that's true. I really do.

— I know you do.

— I don't want you fucking up.

— I know you don't.

— You ain't handle yourself right when you like that. I don't wanna be part of all that.

— Well, you won't have to be … And I handle myself fine.

— You don't, Bow-Be. You just had you some money to dig yourself out of some shit, but you ain't got all that money now.

I didn't answer, letting him know he made his point and could drop it now.

— Aight son. You a grown man, you can take care of your own business.

— All right, Robert Lee, let's not get crazy.

And he laughed his Bob laugh and that was that.

#

We're driving on Vermont below Gage, down where it gets wide and wild.

— When we get there just make the block, I don't want to go in 'less we has to.

Kyle had changed the script, and now wanted to meet at Mac's barbershop. I didn't even know he knew Mac.

— So, what she want this woman?

— Carla's sister?

— Did I meet her once? That the girl you come down here with that time in the Range Rover?

— The one who got blood on your ceiling?

— Yeah.

— No, that was that one I broke out of rehab with, remember? Then her husband called and offered me five hundred dollars if I brought her home.

Robert Lee laughed his little laugh.

— Oh yeah, that's right.

— You don't know the sister. She don't fuck with no dope.

I get down to Century and make a left toward Avalon. South Central's like a warm bath to me, but I always feel Watts in my stomach.

— He thought you might be coming with lawyers or police or some shit, that's why he want me there.

— No, that's not their angle.

And Bob doesn't want to know what their angle is. This isn't showbiz. Down here, knowing sordid details of people's business can get you killed.

Bob's phone rings. He digs it out of his pocket and un-flips it with a grimace. He checks the number.

— Where you at Mac, shop?

Mac starts talking and goes for a minute. Bob listens like it's all bullshit.

— Aight, he there with you? Put him on ... I heard you man, put him on ... Hey son? ... No, no, it's just me and him ... Aight, you sure? ... No, I hear you.

I didn't know what Kyle was saying, I just knew it wasn't good for me.

— What's going on?

Bob made like he didn't hear me.

— Let me talk to him.

— You ain't got to explain to me.

That was to Kyle.

— Bob, give me the phone.

He turns toward the window. I'm the only reason these two even knew each other, but now I'm the odd man out.

— Robert Lee.

— Aight, check in with me later.

— Let me talk to him.

But he just hangs up.

— What are you doing, why didn't you give me the phone?

— Man don't want talk to you. Come on and run me back home.

— What's he doing over at Mac's?

— What you think?

— From Mac?

— What you care, Bow-Be?

I pull over in front of a fried chicken, Chinese food and donuts place and dial Kyle's number. No answer.

— Told you man, he ain't wanna talk to you.

— Where's Mac's place?

— Bow-Be.

— Just take me.

— Bow-Be.

— I just need to talk to Kyle for five minutes. Take me to Mac's, if it all works out, I'll take care of you.

— Bow-Be.

— I'll give you a hundred bucks.

He looks at me like his integrity is worth a lot more than a C-note ... But then the reality of his habit kicks in.

— Suit yourself.

#

When I get to Mac's, Kyle's in front. As soon as he sees me get out, he starts walking fast up Avalon. I chase after him past some used Salvadorian refrigerators for sale on the sidewalk.

— Dude, what are you doing?

That's me calling after him, but he's booking hard, as he talks on the phone.

— Hey, you were supposed to pick me up on 103rd, but I'm walking up Avalon toward 104th so pick me up there ...

He's on the phone with Uber and trying to keep me away.

— Dude ...

— Actually, I'm just going to be walking up Avalon for awhile, so just look for me. You're in a black Camry, right?

— Kyle, what the fuck is going on? Slow down.

But he just speeds up, as we fly past some young brothers in blue, hunkered in front of a boarded-up storefront.

— Bro, why are you running away from me?

He breaks into a half jog and now everyone on the goddamn block is looking at us.

— Kyle!

He turns his head but not his body.

— I got nothing to say to you.

— What is going on?

I'm about twenty feet behind him now.

— Dude, will you stop, this is ridiculous ... Kyle ... Kyle ... Wherever you're going I'll drive you.

He spins around, and sprints right at me screaming, "I know, okay, I fucking know!"

I'm not ready for the intensity of his pain or the wounded animal shriek, but I go right to Carla. She told him I didn't help her, and he's blaming me for her death.

— I know!

He stops right in front of me, and I get my first real look at him. He looks awful, speedball skinny and maggot-colored.

— I know you fucked Lupita. She told me everything ... You fuck your sponsee's girlfriend while he's in rehab? That's the lowest of the low!

But before I even get a chance to swallow the shame I feel something behind me, and what I feel is all over Kyle's face.

— What's goin' on here?

I turn around, and the young cats we just went by are on us, and they don't have to front to look hard.

— Just a little misunderstanding. We're done.

— He don't look done.

A little 5'8" hunk of blue granite tips his chin toward Kyle.

— Look, bra, we're friends with Mac who works in the barbershop.

— Don't "bra" me motherfucka. I don't care who the fuck you friends with. 'Side he just work over here, he ain't from here.

Is this really happening? I'm too old for this shit. I look at the dude and shrug without shrugging. He's not buying it. A black Camry stops about thirty feet up the street.

— That's my Uber.

Kyle heads for the car, leaving me with my new friends.

— You ain't headin' out wich yo boy?

— My car's parked down the street.

— This motherfucker should pay a tariff.

That was the little piece of granite.

— Look, I'm just an old junkie, fellas, I used to go the clinic right there on Avalon back in the day.

— You don't look like no junkie.

— How much money you got on you, bra?

White cats aren't supposed to get fucked with down here because the cops don't like it, but clearly these youngsters didn't get the memo.

— What happened to your eye? Look like someone beat yo' ass already.

I just stand there with absolutely no idea what to say. Blue Granite takes a step toward me.

— We ain't know any Mac.

Oh fuck, this is actually happening.

— What's goin' on, Bow-Be, what takin' you so long?

And there's Robert Lee like the cavalry, just like he was when I crashed into the Buick. He looks at the Crips and immediately knows which one is in charge.

— Hey son.

— He wich you?

— Yeah.

And just like that, it's over. As we walk back to my car Robert Lee shakes his head.

— These youngsters ain't got no sense.

29.

I'm back at the W hotel, and the sheets are crisp and covering half of me. Angie's running the shower with the door open and the steam seeping out into the cool air feels like a wonderful childhood memory, just not one of mine. I didn't expect the return engagement, but get the feeling she wants to keep me as close as possible until she gets her smock. Though closeness is a pretty subjective notion.

When I dropped Robert Lee back on Budlong he said:

— You ain't get that shiner playin' no basketball.

I looked at him in a way that let him know he was right but didn't explain the rest.

— You got an extra bag, Robert Lee?

— I ain't givin' you no bag, Bow-Be.

— Give you fifty bucks for it.

— I ain't givin' you no bag. You wanna fuck up you do that on your own. 'Sides, you ain't want no bag. You just ain't thinkin' right. You shoulda know better than to be fuckin' with Kyle's girl.

For a second I thought he meant Carla, but then realized it was Lupita he was talking about.

Angie comes out of the shower swaddled in terry cloth and drying her hair.

— Using towels I'll never have to wash never ceases to thrill me.

— You wash your own towels?

— I launder from time to time.

I just shook my head.

— I think that's the most normal sex I've ever had with you.

— You sound disappointed.

— I might be.

She looks at herself in the mirror and goes back to drying.

Are you interested in tantra, sweetie? I don't know a damn thing about it, but I'm curious as hell.

— Can't we just have Indian food instead?

After I left Robert Lee I was lost. I didn't know if I would have taken the bag if he had given it to me, or whether I would have done it if I had taken it, but sometimes even the gallows seems preferable to the unknown. That's why when Angie texted asking me if I wanted to come meet her at the W, I felt like the Governor had called with a reprieve.

— That black eye is fabulous. When you walked in I felt it right in my cunt, and please don't tell my therapist I said that.

— You're just a moll at heart.

She smiles and for a second and I think she actually likes me.

— You don't really want me to go Italy with you, do you?

— I wouldn't have mentioned it if I didn't. But you were so ghastly to me at the gallery I may have changed my mind.

— Sorry.

— No, you're not. But that's what I like about you most, you open your mouth and the messy, imperfect truth blurts out.

— Except when I'm lying.

— Right.

She points at my eye with the tip of her English nose.

— I am wondering how you got that, though maybe you shouldn't tell me. What I have in my head is quite fabulous, and I don't want to be let down when I find out you walked into a door.

— All I'll say is you should have seen the other guy.

She comes over and gives the shiner a weightless kiss.

— It really is very Chinatown.

I tried to smile like Nicholson but my eyebrows won't cooperate.

— You're giving me a chance to get in touch with my inner Faye Dunaway.

— Except you fucked your half brother, not your father.

— Really? How do you know I didn't do them both? Maybe I'm Carla's mother as well as her sister.

— If you were Carla's mother you'd be a lot more upset.

Her eyes went from blue pools to green slits.

— I thought we could have at least one encounter where you didn't say something horrible!

She springs up like a shot and storms into the bathroom.

— That was a stupid thing to say, sorry.

She doesn't answer, milking her indignation in private.

— Come on Angie, just give me a pass this one time.

She came flying in with the wind behind her.

— My God, Bobby, how many fucking passes do you need?

It was a good question. But before I could answer, the phone rang with a loud chirp that scared the shit out of both of us. Angie glared at me, like the last hour had never happened, and reached for it.

— Yes, that's fine.
She headed back to the bathroom and called over her shoulder.
— Put your fucking clothes on, Liam's on his way up.
She poked a bare shoulder back out.
— And not a fucking word about Matisse.

30.

— Good to see someone's finally popped you for that cheeky mouth of yours.

There's something about a black eye that makes everyone think they have a right to comment.

— So, what have you two been up to, smells like the deed in here.

We're in the living room of the small suite. Liam's standing in the middle like a captain inspecting the deck.

— Not even a pot of tea, much less something real to drink. You're losing it, sis.

— Shall I call room service?

— No, just point me to the minibar, and I'll have myself a ten quid ounce of Jack.

He shoots me a look like he's a big cat and I'm a ball of yarn.

— You're awfully quiet, Robert. Did you not take not the news well?

— What news?

Liam looks to Angie, as he crosses past her, then down before the tiny fridge like a catcher behind the plate. He comes up with a big yellow can of Boddington's Ale.

— One can never argue with a proper can of Manchester Ale.

— What's he talking about?

That's me to Angie, but Liam doesn't give her any time to answer.

— She really hasn't told you? I thought you'd taken the news in stride and put the boots to her anyway.

I look to Angie for some context, but she just stares at the floor.

— You're out, Robert. You're fired, you're through. Otto's decided to handle the situation himself, so your incompetence is no longer needed.

He pops the top, takes a swig, and sits down on a pale green love seat. Angie moves to the minibar and grabs an eight-dollar Fuji water.

— What's going on?

That's me to her again.

— It's a long, complicated story.

— Give him the short version, luv.

She spins on Liam and hisses,

— Don't!

Then she turns back to me with her gaze focused somewhere to the left of my hip.

— The complex my gallery is in was bought by some Google C.O. something or other and he didn't just raise my rent, he tripled it, and a lot of my assets are tied up with—

— There's no fucking art, Robert ...

Liam had no time for back story.

— Erase it from your brain. There's no drawings, there's no ring, there's no anything. Turns out your friend Kyle has nothing to do with any of this, and if he does we'll handle it in-house. Now we've given you fifteen thousand dollars between us. You can keep twenty-five hundred, but you'll have to give us the back the rest.

— Let him keep five thousand.

— Twenty-five hundred, and the rest comes back.

He was talking to her but looking at me.

— So what, you were just playing me at Musso's?

— I told you the truth at Musso's; I told you Angela hadn't been straight with you.

— Yeah, but you weren't being straight with me either.

— No one's been straight with anyone, least of all you. Did you tell Ange you had taken that five thousand from me? Did you call me to tell me you had taken another ten from her? I don't begrudge you, Robert, but now that we've established that we're all full of shite let's talk straight now, shall we?

— I didn't call Angie because you told me she was lying.

— And you believed him?

She said it like the ingénue in a bad British drama.

— I don't know what I believed.

— But you decided to take the word of a man you'd met for five minutes over a woman who cared about you and gave you fucking money to pay your car note when you didn't have a cent?

It didn't sound good when she put it that way.

— You just assumed I'd been dishonest with you, didn't you?

I'm not sure how she had suddenly ascended to the moral high ground, but I fell right in line, toppling backward into a little ditch of shame.

— What he said made sense to me, or something about your story didn't or maybe the whole thing just kinda freaked me out with you just calling me out of the blue and him walking around naked and

Carla OD'ing in South Central with some mystery dude who turns out to be someone I know and have even more weird shit with than I have with you ...

— Then why did you agree to do it?

— Because I needed the dough.

— Well, now you've got twenty-five hundred dollars for your trouble.

That was Liam.

— And everybody's lied to everybody. At least you got shagged a couple of times, Robert. All in all, I'd say it's been a fairly productive few days.

— I'm not giving you back the money.

— It wasn't my money. It's Otto's and he wants it back.

— Let him keep five thousand.

That was Angie trying to assuage her guilt.

— Twenty-five hundred, and it's more than he deserves. He hasn't done a fucking thing but eat creamed spinach and soil the sheets at this hotel.

— I found Kyle.

Angie jerks like she's been shocked. Even Liam takes a step back, though he doesn't move.

— Well, why didn't you say so earlier, Robert? That's rather pertinent information.

— What's pertinent about it? You said he's got nothing to do with it.

— Does he have the key?

That's Angie.

— I don't know, I didn't ask him.

— Well, what did you ask him?

Liam.

— I didn't get a chance to ask him anything.

— Why not?

— Because I didn't, we didn't get a chance to talk.

— But you know where he is?

— Not exactly, but I can get in touch with him.

— Fine, give us his number and you can keep five thousand dollars.

— No.

— No what?

— I'm not giving you his number.

— Unless what?

— Unless nothing.

— Don't be an idiot, Robert. We're going to find your friend one way or another. Now give me the number before I change my mind.

— All right. Let's go.

— Where, to Kyle?

— No, to the bank, so I can give you the money back. You're not getting anywhere fucking near Kyle.

— Bobby, please, there's no need for any of this. Just give us Kyle's number and I'll talk to Otto about you keeping the money.

I spin on Angie, my shame and guilt flash-fried into rage.

— I don't want your fucking money. And next time you feel the ache just call your fucking brother!

31.

I'm up on Jeffrey's floor at DreamWorks, and it feels like Dante's seventh circle. In fact, the whole damn campus is like Tuscany in hell; a corporate sprawl of ochre-colored villas spread around a bloodless piazza with ping-pong tables.

There was enough pressure on this pitch when I had my next few months of rent paid, but I had to get all stupid and have Liam follow me directly from the hotel to the bank, where I handed him back all his dough like I had integrity. Now I don't just need to nail the pitch, so I can settle the score with Katzenberg. I need it to pay the bills.

On the drive over, I had the following conversation with Nick, Andrew's second in command, who called as I headed down Barham.

— Hey dude.

— Hey man.

— You excited for the pitch?

— I'm appropriately sickened.

— Don't worry, dude, you're going to kill it.

Then he turned down the radio.

— Dude, Wood just texted me. He says he can't make it.

— What do you mean?

— I don't know, he says he can't come, but we should go ahead without him.

— It's his idea.

— I know.

A wave of panic came over me. When you've been a fuckup most of your life you always think you're the one in trouble, or at least was responsible for it.

— Is he okay?

— I don't know. He's been acting a little weird lately.

I just let that one lay there. I didn't know how much Nick knew and it didn't seem like an ideal time to dig into Wood's relapse.

— He really wants us to go ahead without him?

— That's what he said. If we don't see Jeffrey today we'll have to wait at least two months.

— I can't wait two months.

— I know, shit. None of this is going to look good after what happened on Pringle.

— What's Pringle?

— A movie we have in post.

— About potato chips?

— No, that's the lead character's name. He's an android, an android hit man who's accidentally implanted with the personality of a six-year-old girl. We were shooting in Atlanta and Wood got into some weird thing there where he reported his car stolen, but then it was found in this fucked-up neighborhood with two black women driving it ...

I knew this story wasn't going to end well. I just didn't know how not well.

— They said he had given it to them with his credit card to go get some barbecue and bring it back to his hotel room, but he said he'd never met them. It got ugly, and there was a physical altercation at the police station and the story got in the papers. DreamWorks was one of the co-producers. So, it's already a little iffy with them.

— Well, what do you want to do?

He took a long beat.

— I say we just go in there and kick ass. You're the man.

#

Conference rooms make me physically ill, and I can't remember anything good ever happening in one. You want your pitch to seem like a story around the campfire, but a conference room makes it feel like the deposition of a class action lawsuit. Even the walk over from the waiting area is like a stroll to the gallows. The psychotically pleasant assistant leading us to some sterile rectangle specifically built for men to say "no" in.

Nick and I walk in. We're joking with Destitrino and the dumpy kid, but our laughter has the squashed uneasiness of doom.

We're seated at a long horizontal table, and asked if we'd like a beverage, the showbiz version of cigarette and blindfold. There are three chairs on our side, and one on the other. That's the judgment chair, aka Jeffrey's throne. At the moment it's empty, but there's a can of Diet Coke and a glass of five perfect ice cubes waiting for the king. I take a breath and look around for something to hold onto, something that isn't sleek, mirrored or chrome. Destitrino and the dumpy kid have taken seats behind us against the wall. That way if our pitch goes off the rails and explodes, they'll be far enough away to not get any of our failure on their clothes.

I turn to Nick and say something about him feeling free to chip in when the double glass doors push open and there he is, the teeny little boy-man with the too-big head.

Nick and I stand like you would for a dignitary, even though we're supposedly just shaking hands. Destitrino gets up and does the introductions. When he says, "This is Bobby Zorn" I wait for Jeffrey to say: "I know Bobby" or "Bobby and I go back a long way," but he gives me nothing, not even a crumb. He just offers a vacant smile that says, "I don't remember you, and if I do, it is of no use to you now."

But I'm not going down so easy. I look him in the eye and say "It's good to see you, man," like we have history together and both know it, but the words bounce off him like he's wearing a bulletproof vest. He sits down, pours his Diet Coke, and I watch it fall majestically over the perfect ice.

#

Please, God I do not believe in, God who shows up at the strangest times, who supposedly has my best interests at heart; I am turning the wheel over to you. Now drive this fucking junker across the burning bridge of my insanity.

Actually, you know what? Fuck this pitch. I'm not going to do some dog and pony show for a guy whose little ogre movie I helped donkeyize into a zillion dollar franchise, but who doesn't even have the decency to acknowledge he knows who I am. *Okay, Zorn, relax. That kind of thinking is definitely not going to help.* The hero always comes from obscurity. That's not a can of Diet Coke on that table, it's a golden chalice, all you have to do is grab it. All you have to do is relax and tell this freaky little billionaire a simple story about a boy who has no music in his life but learns to find it.

Destitrino says some nonsense about loving the project, and then boom, the gate pops open. I'm like a downhill racer at the Olympics, skiing for the gold. I slalom through the first few gates okay, but in two minutes all I can hear is the strange sound of my own voice in a room full of strangers. I try to go off script with a wild riff about kids and narcissistic parents, and jar myself back to the present, but I just end up deeper in the weeds. I can feel the air seeping out of Nick, as Katzenberg's smile gets more and more glazed.

There's no chitchat at the end, no questions and no concerns. Just an empty can of Diet Coke.

In the elevator Nick says, "He's tough, but it wasn't as bad as you think." Not the first words you want to hear from your producer. "He might still buy it. Wood should have been there." I just smiled at him cryptically. It was over, all of it.

32.

The wind is back to blowing like Big Jay McNeely as I stumble down Santa Monica Boulevard trying to remember my name. You want to shed your first world overalls and get a glimpse of what it's like to live on level three, travel by foot down Santa Monica near Wilton when night starts to fall. Out here the mannequins got big old booties, and the pupusa lady fires up her flat top, settling in for an all-night vigil of greasy cheese and pickled cabbage. Across the way, my favorite Guatemalan couple is getting set to call it a night. It don't take long to go from the Mayan empire to slingin' roasted peanuts out of a red wheelbarrow on Western, or from an overall deal at Disney to working for free on pipe-dream projects that get torn up like losing lottery tickets and thrown in the air. Too bad you can't just hate yourself back to success 'cause I'd be living large.

I buy three dollars' worth of peanuts, and they throw in a gold tooth smile for free. Now I'm sitting in the Hollywood Forever Cemetery crackin' shells amongst the headstones and listening to the wind in the palms. I take out my phone in the graveyard half-light, looking to it like a magic eight ball. Do something phone, say something, reveal me to myself, give me succor, save me. I check my inbox just in case I've read the Katzenberg thing completely wrong. Orbitz has great fares to Baltimore, but I see nothing about getting my career back. I go to "photos" and sneak a peek at a pic I took of the portrait of Carla in the gold smock. She stares at me like I'm the only man left in the world. I enlarge it, getting rid of Otto, and moving in on her face until my screen is just half a mouth, half a nose and one slate gray eye. I'm sorry baby, I'm sorry I didn't just do what you asked and go down to the desert with you and see you through to the other side. I pussy'd out and played it safe and now we both got nothing.

My phone rings, startling me so badly it goes flying out of my hand. I go and dig the ringing slab out of the grass and look at the number. It's not Unknown Artists, but it is a 424 and I don't think it's the dentist I owe. Could it be showbiz calling with the golden ticket? Could the pitch gods be merciful and shock us all with a yes? Could some Century City agent have heard of my triumph and want to sign me before I blow up big? I need good news so bad my

mouth goes dry.
— Hello
— Is this za screenwriter?
— It is.
— This is Otto Schlein.

33.

— You feel it like negative space in a great painting. You feel vat *isn't*, and zis intense sense of vat *isn't* only makes you more aware of vat *is*. And now you remember things not as they were, but as you need them to be. This image of love as a heart is an obvious one, the heart, a simple engine, beating, keeping the time of your existence, yet to me a far more pertinent image for love is a wound, for the wound is an even deeper red than the heart.

That's Otto Schlein waxing his version of sentimental. We're tucked into a corner two top at The Prince, a Koreatown hangout carved into the cellar of The Windsor Court, the kind of old Hollywood building where silent film stars did twisted things to underage girls. Schlein turns his head to profile, the two-day stubble on his big lantern jaw rough enough to grate cheese.

— Have you ever been in love, screenwriter?

— Yeah, I been in love. Or at least nearby.

— Next town over?

— Same town. Different street.

— Vas she good for you?

— Which one?

— The one you loved the most.

— No. At least not while it was happening.

— I have no need for a woman who is good for me. None.

— How about alive, do you need her to be alive?

A squat Korean waitress with a valley accent and East L.A. eyebrows comes to see what we're drinking. Otto orders a Harvey Wallbanger.

— Would you like one?

— No, I'll have an Old-Fashioned.

I have no idea what's in an Old-Fashioned, but if he's having a Harvey Wallbanger, I'm having an Old-Fashioned. The waitress smiles, the diamond stud in her nose twinkling like a distant star.

— I prefer addicts to drunks.

— I'm not a drunk.

— I'm not saying you are. I'm just saying I prefer addicts.

Maybe that was his way of trying to snuggle up to me, but it puts me on guard.

— So, how come you called?

— What do you mean?

— Liam told me I should forget the whole thing, that you didn't want anything to do with me.

— As I advised him to. But I hope you will keep vat is said here between you and I.

— Sure, I got no allegiance to them at this point.

He gave me a smile that Fassbinder would have put on the poster.

— You knew her, correct?

— Carla?

He nodded.

— Yeah, but not well.

I couldn't imagine she'd had ever told him about our little near adventure, and I sure as hell wasn't going to.

— She was beautiful, no?

— She was more than beautiful.

Not exactly the comment of a stranger nor was the way I said it, but luckily he was more interested in what he had to say.

— Yes, beautiful and more than beautiful. You would think such a gift would be a blessing, but instead it was a curse.

He reached into the breast pocket of his jacket, took out a half-eaten bar of fancy dark chocolate and pushed it toward me like a pack of smokes.

— No thanks, tryin' to quit.

He broke off a black square and popped it in his mouth.

— Liam and Angie are not to be trusted. No one from that family is.

— Wish you'd have told me that a week ago.

— What did they tell you about me?

— What's it matter? They're not to be trusted.

— Ah, snappy dialogue. Very good screenwriter. I would expect no less.

— I haven't heard anything about you except you were with Angie, traded her in for Carla and that you and Carla had some kind of intense, volatile situation.

— You heard this from Liam?

— Yeah, as well as some other slightly unflattering shit, and then Angie told me not to mention the Matisse, so I don't know what that's about.

He studied me a moment.

— That's a very nice bruise around your eye. The colors. Reminds me of Sonia Delaunay. You know her work?

— No.

— She could be your sister. Lived in France but born in the Ukraine. Are your people from Ukraine?

— On my father's side.

— I'm not surprised, you look just like her, especially the eyes.

— Ukrainian Jews got those violin player eyes.

I wasn't sure what I meant by that, but he seemed to.

— So, you going to tell me about the art?

— Don't worry about the art. We have other things to discuss.

— Oh yeah. Screenwriting or junkie chasing?

— I need no screenwriting, the movie is being lived.

It was the truest thing I had heard all week. The waitress comes back with the drinks. Mine has a cherry. Shots of heroin never came with cherries.

— To grief. The only thing realer than art.

It was a corny line, but you can't fault a guy for trying.

— So why did you tell Angie and Liam to can me?

— Vat does it matter?

— Well, I've been running all over the city chasing this key.

— What key?

— You don't know about the key?

He gives me a bug-eyed look of bewilderment. Then laughs.

— Of course, I know about the key. Drink your drink. I want you a bit drunk, so I can get you to do as I wish.

— Dude, I just gave Liam all your dough back, you're not going to have any trouble getting me to do as you wish. 'Less you want me to kill someone.

— No, not yet.

I looked at him to see if he was serious, but he just took another sip of his drink, then tasted it a second time on his upper lip.

— So, how well do you know this Kyle?

— Well.

— You think you are a good judge of his character?

— I do.

— Do you think he vas capable of killing her?

— You mean like giving her a hot shot? Absolutely not.

— You don't think he could have purposely overdosed her?

— I just told you. No. Besides, why would he?

— For money.

— No. He's not that kind of junkie, he's just a sad kid. He's an artist, a good one, I mean he'll do what he needs to do, but he's not a killer or a thief.

— Perhaps not a killer, but he is absolutely a thief.

— Why, because he stole your girl?

— Because he stole my art.

— What art?

— The Matisse smock.

— I thought it was Carla's.

— Yes, but it vas kept at my house in a locked cabinet. She vas the only other person who knew the combination. The house I am staying in has a surveillance camera outside. She can be seen leaving with a small valise and getting into the passenger side of a car. It would make sense that person driving that car vas your friend Kyle.

— It could have been anybody.

— It vas one week before she died, and they were living in motels and using drugs together.

He turned his head and stared out into the black hum of the bar. When his eyes came back to me he looked like someone else.

— But that is not all she took.

— What, the Hockneys?

— The Hockneys are fakes. They are for selling to Arabs.

That threw me a little, but I tried not to show it.

— What else did they take?

— This is between me and your friend.

— You want to talk to him?

— Yes ... In person.

He pulled the orange slice from his drink and ate it, rind and all.

— I am doing him a favor, believe me. There are other people who have an interest in vat vas taken who are losing patience. And they have no warm spot for Carla or your friend.

I didn't really know what he was talking about, but it didn't sound good.

— So, what's the pay scale for all this? I could use a little dough.

— Bring me your friend, you'll get money.

— What about the key?

— I want it. Unless your friend has already used it, which is why

I want you to bring him to me.

We were down to the crux of it, so I knew I could dictate the terms.

— I'll give it a shot, but I'm going to need thousand bucks to start.

He dug into his pocket and tossed some bills on the table.

— Here's few hundred to keep you out of trouble.

So much for dictating the terms.

— But you're going to take care of me for real if I get you in a room with Kyle?

— Worry not, screenwriter. If things go well you will have marks in your pocket ... But you are going to do it either way.

— Oh yeah, why's that?

— Because. She's in your blood now too.

She'd been there for a while.

34.

The street wants to be black and lawless, but there's so much action in K-town the nights are brighter than the days. I'm pulled over at a hydrant on Sixth near Berendo. A lone streetlamp pours white through the windshield. I keep going back to her face like a flask.

A big blast of wind nearly lifts my toy car off the ground, but it doesn't even budge the hair on the heads of the Korean hipsters. I start wondering about how Carla might have sounded when she came, and decide she'd have broken into peals of laughter, and then not wanted to be touched for an hour. I see her smoking with the sheet pulled up like Mrs. Robinson, shutting you out cold after laying it all at your feet. Like a drug that gets you hooked for life after one shot, just one taste and you were instantly Icarus-ized, flapping around for the rest of your days with a pair of melted wings. Fuck. I'm starting to lose my mind a little, but I'm not enjoying it nearly as much as I used to.

And then: *buzz buzz buzz*, my phone starts vibrating on the console like that device from Pollo Loco that lets you know your food's ready. I want it to magically be Kyle, but I get a strong feeling it's Angie.

Neither. It's Andrew Wood. Good, I need a distraction.

— Hey man.

— I hear the pitch went amazing.

— Who told you that?

— Nick.

— Nick said it went amazing?

— No, but he said it wasn't as bad as you thought. Dude, I'm really sorry I didn't make it, the morning just got away from me. You ever heard of Robot Sushi?

— No.

— They make a lot of content in the Occulus Rift space, but they want to move into movies. Or move movies to where they are? I ran into their CEO at Whole Foods and told him about Jukebox, and he *loved* it. Didn't hurt that he was rocking an Elvis T-shirt.

— What were you doing at Whole Foods? Picking up yoga teachers?

— Getting some green juice, I've been feeling a little run-down.

— Just add more coke to your shot, you'll be fine.

— Okay, I deserved that, I dropped the ball, but the truth is, my work was sort of done and I didn't really need to be there. And by the way, I'm not shooting anything.

He said it like that was proof there was nothing to worry about.

— What are you doing right now?

— I'm driving through Koreatown feeling ridiculous.

— Well, turn around and come to my place.

— Where's your place?

— Lake Hollywood, in back of the sign. I'm having a small get together and Yonah Melber's here and he's been up for thirty-six hours and he wants to write you a check.

— For what?

— Don't worry about it. He's got a lot of ideas and all of them need fleshing out.

— He's going to pay me to flesh out ideas?

— Dude, just get here. He's got his checkbook open and he can barely put two sentences together.

— Well, there you go. That's the way all great movies begin.

— Funny, just get here.

— I can't right now, I got some shit I got to handle.

— Dude, I'm not calling you at midnight because I want you to see my iguana. Yonah Melber is here and he's in a very good mood. The portal is open. Something good is going to happen tonight.

— What's your address?

— I'll text it to you.

— Just tell it to me. I don't want you hanging up and disappearing into a k-hole.

— 3143 La Suvida Drive 90068.

— Don't tell me the zip code, then I'll forget the address.

— I'll just text it to you.

— Tell it to me and text it to me.

— I told you, 3143 La Suvida Drive. Park in the driveway behind Yonah's Tesla. If there's no spots, just park at the bank on Barham and Uber up the hill.

— What?

— Just park somewhere. And don't get blown away, the wind is like a theme park ride. And we should talk about a wind movie. Real but metaphoric, you track the lead's emotional journey by whether the wind is in his face or at his back. We'll call it The Weather Inside.

— Good title.

— Great. We'll pitch it to Yonah. He'll love it. Hurry up and get here before he collapses. Oh, and dude, just so you know. Some of the people here are doing drugs.

#

The wind is howling through the hill streets and the palm fronds are whipping around like helicopter blades. It sounds like a Vietnam movie. Woods' house is an old one-story Spanish with black iron gates on the windows, but something tells me it's more to keep him in than other people out. I make my way up the tile steps, leaning into the wind like an old-school fullback, then I ring the bell. I hear nothing, so I rap hard on the door. About ten seconds later it swings open on a six-foot blonde wearing nothing but a Kevin Durrant jersey and red ski boots.

So, it's going to be that kind of night.

— Who are you?

— I think you're supposed to ask that before you open the door.

— Fucking wind, man, I'll never get used to it.

I register the Russian accent, as I step inside.

— You from somewhere windless?

— What?

— You said you'll never get used to the wind.

She stares at me blankly through yellow bangs.

— What the fuck, man, I just met you.

I can't tell if she's serious, so I laugh and say, "You're funny."

— You don't even know.

She reaches back with a long rope arm and takes my hand, leading me up three ninety-year-old tile steps and back down two into the living room. Wood clocks me being towed in and calls from a green suede couch.

— I knew you and Oksana would get each other.

— What's up, man? Nice house.

He's got a cigarette in his mouth and is holding it like someone who only smokes when they do coke.

— She's read everyone. All the Russians, but also Pushkin, Gorky and Turgenev.

— Those are all Russians.

Oksana spins on me like a cobra.

— Have you read Turgenev?

— No, but I've heard of him, so that's sort of like reading him.

She drops my hand and clip-clops over to a brunette laid out on a crimson sofa-chaise and moves in for a cuddle. I don't know what drugs she's doing, but opiates don't go with ski boots, so I would say speed or art school.

#

The coffee table is a sprawling inch-thick slab of glass on four industrial rubber wheels. On it is a small fortune in coffee table books, a vase of white roses, a Plexiglas box filled with cut-up dollar bills, an autographed framed photo of a little boy posing with Evel Knievel, a roll of Reynolds wrap, and a torn, open five-pack of Bic lighters.

And sitting front and center are the empties. Only in this case, they are not beer bottles, but sheets of aluminum foil, the long black ashy scars like tribal tattoos. Clearly Wood has worked on his junk smoking technique and raised his game, but there must be some coke around too, because he's chewing his cigarette as he smokes. As for Yonah Melber, he's running his hands through a thick, lustrous shrub of black hair and there's a thin sheen of coke sweat on his beautiful olive skin. I've done a lot of drugs in my life, but they never made me look like I just stepped out of a *GQ* version of the Old Testament.

— I need five set pieces. In each of these it has to be two trailer moments. That's what I need. What you do between those set pieces is your business, but if a scene is not funny, scary, emotional or sexy, I cut it. You write one like that for me, then you can write one for yourself.

Clearly good looks do not keep one from talking nonsense.

— All right, dude, but what's the movie about?

— I don't care. That's for you to figure out. I just need the set pieces and the trailer moments.

— You like a nice set piece, huh?

— I need five.

A set piece is a large scene in a movie that you hopefully remember, like the food fight in *Animal House*, the bar scene in *Star*

Wars, or the high school dance in *Back To The Future*.
— So, I can write about whatever I want?
— Yes, as long as it's commercial.
— And that's your strategy for winning Oscars?
— No, the ones you write for *you* win the Oscars. The ones you write for him pay for the ones you write for you.

That was Wood, playing interpreter.
— Unless you think you can write my Mossad movie?
— What's your Mossad movie?
— It's a movie based on my Uncle's time in the Mossad. You know what Mossad is?
— Yeah, it's like the Israeli CIA.
— It's the world's most lethal killing machine.
— Okay, but it's still like the CIA.
— The CIA? The CIA is like Boy Scouts next to Mossad. You want to know how the movie opens?
— The Mossad movie?
— What do you think I am talking about?!

He delivered the line with a weird cocaine shriek.
— Sure, man, how does it open?
— We are in a safe house outside of Beirut. A family is eating dinner. Suddenly the door is kicked open and the family is gunned down with six shots. Only six, not all this machine gun fire like *Scarface*. Six shots. Three killers. Two shots each.
— They kill the wife and kids too?
— Absolutely.
— How old are the kids?
— Young. Then the leader, Avram, the character who is my Uncle, comes over to the father of the family, and his head is split open from a perfect kill shot, brains all over. He kneels down over the body, picks up some of the brains and eats them. Then he turns to the other two who are baby faces and says, "Either you eat their brains, or they will eat yours." That's how the movie opens. You want to write it?
— No.
— Why not?
— Because I don't write those kinds of movies.

One of the Russian girls lets out a shriek and I jump. I glance over and they're pretzeled up watching something on an iPad, one pair of ear buds between them. The brunette puts her cigarette in the blonde's mouth and calls out happily, "Russian TV will rot your brain."

— Those ski boots are a strong look.

That's me to Wood, but he's staring at his phone like he wants to eat it. He turns to Yonah.

— He just got on the freeway. He'll be here soon.

You don't have to have shot dope in every gas station bathroom on Vermont to know Wood's talking about a dealer. Now, he turns to me.

— What'd you say?

— Just commenting on the ski boot as house slipper look.

— Yeah, we were talking about going to Banff and she got so excited she put my ski boots on.

— Nice you guys can share shoes.

I feel some dark Tel Aviv energy to my left, and turn to it. Yonah is staring at me and sucking hard on a Marlboro light.

— You know, if you gave me the choice between a great movie with a bad poster and a bad trailer and a bad movie with a great poster and a great trailer I would take the bad movie every time.

He looks at me like I'm meaningless, and like what I do is meaningless. Then he crosses his legs, leans back, and takes another drag.

— Go ahead, pitch me an idea. Come on, what do you want to write for me?

— You want me to *pitch* you an idea? I thought you were going to pitch me.

— No, pitch me something. I want to buy. Just make something up. How about a bank robbery movie, I want to do one of those.

— You want me to make up a bank robbery movie right now?

— Sure, or a comedy or a horror movie, whatever you want.

Some Russian techno music comes on out of nowhere, and the Ruski chicks get up and start to dance. One barefoot, one in ski boots. Yonah raises his voice above the music.

— Go ahead, do it, pitch me something. I like it, I write you a check.

He looks at me like he just fired a pistol at my feet and expects me to dance. And somehow, I'm back here once again. Not in this particular room, just this particular land, that strange, nauseating land where someone is asking me to *prove it.*—Go ahead, do it, pitch me something. I like it, I write you a check. Go ahead, Zorn, show us, sing for us. Get up there and pull gold bars out of your ass. I don't want to be here. I don't want to be anywhere.

— Sorry man I don't have a movie to pitch you ... But let me get a hit off the foil and maybe something will come to me.

I say it super casual like it's no big deal. Wood wasn't expecting that.

— You sure that's a good idea?

— It's fine. It's just a hit off the foil. I'm not going to OD on that. They look at me, and I look at them.

— Okay, but there's nothing left. Dude's on his way.

— You want coke? It's probably better for pitching anyway.

That's Yonah being generous.

— No, coke just makes me shit and clean the house. Just give me the straw.

— I told you we don't have anything.

I reach for the straw and begin to unroll it. Its innards are filled with the brown gray stain of solidified smoke. I pick a lighter off the table and hold it under the steeply tilted foil. Wood looks at me like I'm performing black magic.

— You can smoke the straw?

I hit the lighter and the smoke comes up at me like an obedient genie. I purse my lips and suck it in. Wood and Yonah look at me like we're in a cartoon and I just swallowed nitroglycerin. Only I don't blow up, I just spark the lighter and hit it again. The smoke is sickening and familiar, like someone dipped a soldering iron in vinegar and put it to the back of my throat. I take a pause to consider what I've done. Not just in this moment, but with my life.

— I have to go.

— What, why?

I get up, looking down on Yonah.

— It was nice to meet you, dude. If you're serious about figuring out something to do together, call me in the daytime and we can put some actual thought into it.

— Where are you going?

— And just so you know, it's a real thing. Writing a movie is a real thing. Telling a story is a real thing. You may think it's all about getting people into the theatre, but it's not. What happens once they're there matters, too.

It's my big junkie Mr. Smith Goes to Hollywood moment, but Wood doesn't even hear it. He's looking down at his phone. "He's here."

He heads for the door and I go with him. I half wave to Yonah, then call back to the Russians over my shoulder, "See you ladies."

I can already feel myself a full octave lower from the dope. As I hit the front entrance, Wood opens the door, and some dude in a hoodie walks in saying "It's too windy for this shit." The voice sounds oddly familiar. The hood comes off and I look at his face. It's Kyle.

35.

I'm sitting in a booth at the Bob's Big Boy on Riverside. I just puked in the bathroom and I'm trying to focus on the part of me that feels really awful, not the part that feels really good. As for Kyle, he was in the next stall fixing while I was heaving, but now he's ripped, sitting across from me with a double-decker hamburger in front of him. I feel like I'm going to throw up again, but I really want a bite.

— Eat your burger and let's get out of here. You're way too high to be in public.

When I saw him at Wood's house I was ready for him to storm out, or make a scene, but instead he was all happy to see me like Lupita and what went down in Watts had never happened. Now he's sitting across from me higher than Jesus on the cross.

— You okay?

— Good.

He wasn't good, and neither was I.

— How do you know Andrew Wood?

— Rodney put me in touch with him.

Rodney was an actor in the program who was constantly relapsing.

— Has anyone tried to get in touch with you? Anyone out of the ordinary?

— No. I haven't been findable.

— Well, I found you, it's not like you're in Africa.

— Oh, I'm in Africa.

His head went to his chest like a bad actor playing a junkie on TV.

— I'm so in Africa.

— I need to talk to you about Carla.

He brings the burger to his mouth and it's like watching time-lapse photography in reverse. Dope is funny that way. A minute takes a day and twenty years takes a minute. I reach over and pinch a French fry even though I know I'm just going to puke it up.

— I need you to tell me what happened.

— I'm eating my hamburger.

— No, you're not, you're holding it, you haven't taken one bite.

— Because you won't stop talking.

He was slurring his words together like a clarinet player.

— Bro, you're way too high to be out in public. Kyle ... Kyle ... Kyle ... Dude, you can't be this high in here, the cops eat in places like this.

The burger falls, hitting his plate with a thud.

— All right, come on, we're getting out of here.

— No, I'm cool. Let me just do some coke and wake up.

— Let's just go to my place.

— No, I don't want to go to your place.

He starts trying to rebuild his burger, dragging Thousand Island along the red Formica.

— How big a fucking shot did you do?

He gives me a small laugh like it's funny.

— Bro, seriously, we need to get out of here ...

— Just let me do some coke. Jesus, man.

He reaches into his jeans and pulls out a tiny blue ziplock plump with coke.

— What are you, fucking crazy? At least go to the bathroom.

— No one cares, it's the valley.

— Dude, put it away.

He digs into his shirt and pulls out the silver chain he's got around his neck. There's a small gold key hanging from it like a crucifix. He dips it into the little bag like a coke spoon and brings it to his nose. I'm so pissed he's doing coke in the middle of Bob's Big Boy, it takes a second to realize what I'm looking at.

— Is that it?

— Is what it?

— Kyle please, just be straight with me, you don't know what I've been through looking for this thing,

— What thing?

I try to stay calm but it's hard, even with a couple toots off the foil in me.

— That, that's the key to the storage space, right?

He looks up, his eyes now opened by the coke.

— What are you talking about?

— Please dude don't fuck with me right now, I can't handle it.

— I think that waiter is watching us.

I look over and some young busboy is putting silverware down on the next table.

— No he's not. Kyle, just talk to me, Where'd you get that key?

He looks at me but says nothing.
— It that Carla's key?
His eyes go funny, like he's a mute.
— Is it that key to the storage space, please man, just tell me.
— I don't know.
— What do you mean you don't know, what's it a key to?
He stares at me, then looks down like he's about to say something important, but doesn't. Then he springs up like a jack in the box, and heads for the door.
— Kyle!
Now I'm up too, chasing him through the 50s red leatherette. I catch a hard look from a lean, black fry cook which makes me scramble back and throw a twenty on the table.
I catch up to him ten yards out the door in front of the Big Boy statue and its crazy dipsy-do cowlick.
— What is wrong with you?
He's got his phone out.
— Who are you calling? Are you calling Uber, I'll drive you. Kyle ... Put the fucking phone away. What happened with Carla? Did some shit go down? Dude, I'm fucking talking to you!
I grab the phone out of his hands and he throws a wild punch that catches a piece of my jaw. I throw him to the cement and his phone goes flying. He starts to cry.
— Dude, WHAT IS GOING ON?
He makes little animal sounds and gets to his feet.
— Kyle ... Dude, it's okay.
He cries like a little kid. I put my hand on his back and keep it there. It's just me, him and Big Boy.
— She was wearing it.
— What?
The words come out between sobs.
— She wore it around her neck. I just took it to have something of hers. I wasn't there when it happened, I swear. I went to get cigarettes. There was nothing I could do.
— Dude it's okay, just calm down.
— There was nothing I could do!
— Everything okay here?
I turn to the voice and two young cops, one Latino and one Asian, are standing there.
— Yeah, hey officer, he's just upset.

— Everything okay with you, sir?

That's the Asian cop addressing Kyle. He sounds a bit like George Takei.

— He's just upset about his girl.

— Did I ask you?

He gives me the hall monitor look, then takes it back to Kyle.

— Sir, are you okay?

Somehow Kyle mutters "Yeah, I'm fine."

— Have you been drinking?

The Latino cop has moved a few feet away to some kind of academy-trained strategic position. Just those few steps and I know we're fucked. I probably shouldn't talk, but I can't help it.

— He's had a few, but I'm driving, and I haven't. His girl broke up with him, he's just brokenhearted.

— You're not helping yourself by talking.

I know enough to not say "sorry."

— Sir, are you drunk?

Kyle looks at the cop, his eyes ringed with tears

— A little … I'm just really sad.

The cop looks at Kyle, then looks at his partner. Maybe they're nice guys, maybe they're hungry, maybe they just dealt with a couple of knuckleheads even dumber than us, but whatever the reason, they let us go, and we wander off into a red neon haze. When we reach the car, I puke so hard it takes me down to one knee. I wipe my mouth with my sleeve and sit down in the driver's seat with just one thought in my head.

I want more dope.

36.

I'm not going to shoot anything, just the occasional toot or two off the foil until this whole Carla thing gets settled. If you want to catch a junkie, you need to think like a junkie, only I already do think like a junkie, and besides, the junkie I'm trying to catch is right next to me.

— Dude, you cracked the screen on my phone.

Kyle's sitting in one of the three chairs in my living room. If I solve this thing I'm going to buy a couch.

— I can't believe you did that. You're buying me a new one.

I've got the foil in front of me and a pot of strong coffee, my version of an impromptu speedball. I've only taken one more hit, but it made a real impression on me. I don't know if it's woken up the beast, but I need to get this Schlein business straightened out quick 'cause in about seventy-two hours, there's a good chance my life is going to be totally out of control.

— You didn't drive Carla over to Otto's place?

— I'm serious about the phone.

— Bro, you got to tell me the truth about this shit.

— About what?

— About what I'm asking you.

— I don't know what you're asking me.

— I'm asking you if you drove Carla to Otto Schlein's house?

— No, she drove.

— To his place?

— No, everywhere. She always drove, and fast.

I got a quick flash of Carla in a silk scarf driving a mid-60s Ferrari through Rome.

— Can I smoke crack in here?

— No, absolutely not.

I put the lighter to the foil and smoke the last little tail of my hit, and then, while holding it in, say,

— As your ex-sponsor I don't advise it.

That makes him smile, despite himself.

— Let me just smoke it in the bathroom. Someone gave me a twenty. I want to get rid of it.

— Just have a cup of coffee.

— I don't want coffee.

He was back to just being professional-junkie-high and not doing nosedives like at Big Boy.

— You know who Otto Schlein is, right?

The name gave him a twitch.

— Yeah. I know who he is.

— He wants to talk to you.

— About what?

— He thinks you robbed him. Or drove *her* to rob him.

— Well, I didn't.

— Kyle, tell me the truth, I want to help you, but I can't unless you're straight with me.

— You don't want to help me. You want to do what's good for you. That's how you are. You're a selfish asshole, it's part of your charm ... What did she steal?

— You tell me.

— I don't know.

— Yes, you do.

— I swear, I don't.

I get up, head over to the little table by my front door and grab the envelope I laid there when we came in. I unwrap the red string as I walk back over and hand him the photo of Otto and Carla.

— That. What she's wearing.

He looks at the photo. It yanks the breath out of him. It's so fucking intimate I look away to give him some privacy.

— It's a Matisse ballet costume.

— I know. That's him, that's Otto Schlein?

— Yeah. Pretty German, huh?

He stares at the photo some more, just in case it hasn't made him sick enough already.

— You don't happen to have that robe stashed away in a drawer somewhere, do you?

He shakes his head.

— How do you know about it?

— She told me. Showed me a picture of it online. She said it was hers, and he had it, but he wouldn't give it to her.

He puts the picture down like a too-strong drink.

— I need to go to the bathroom.

— Bro, don't do a shot right now.

He stands up but stays where he is.

— We were supposed to go over there the next day and get it. She told me she wanted it back, so she could sell it and move back to Europe, but I guess she'd already gone and got it without me.

It's never fun finding out someone you're in love with lied to you.

— I think it's in a storage space. That's what the key you've got is for, or that seems to be the general consensus. Did she have a storage space?

— Yeah.

— You know where it is?

— No.

— She didn't mention a number, a part of town, anything?

He's back to head shaking.

— Do you have any of her stuff, her papers, a journal?

— No.

— You don't have her phone. Why didn't you take her phone?

— She just OD'd. You know what it's like to have someone die on you, don't you? I was trying to bring her back! I wasn't thinking about her phone.

I got a strong whiff of the Snooty and that room, and Kyle frantically shaking Carla like a rag doll.

— We got to find that storage space. You know her e-mail address?

— Yeah, but not her password.

— But you took some of her clothes, and her bag, right?

— Yeah.

— But you didn't take her phone?

— I forgot it. I wanted to go back for it, but I was scared. And Robert Lee said not to.

— You went right to Robert Lee?

— Yeah. We had done everything and I needed to cop.

— What did he say?

— He said he was sorry, and asked me whose name the room was in.

— Hers?

— Of course. I don't have a credit card.

I let out a big exhale. I could feel his grief and wanted him to know I felt it. Then I picked up the sheet of foil to see if there was anything left, or if it was all ash.

— What are you doing?

I answered by not answering.

— When did you start using?

— About five minutes before you walked into that dude's house.

— You mean tonight?

I nodded and put the flame to the foil. It burped up a measly little gasp of smoke.

— You don't have a habit?

— No, why do you think I'm throwing up?

— Stop now.

— I will, don't worry. I got two or three days.

— That's what I used to tell you.

— I know.

— I'm going to smoke that crack.

— Dude, don't, I can't have the situation deteriorate to crack right now. And besides, you hate crack.

— I know, but what am I going to do with it?

— Flush it down the toilet.

— Have you ever flushed drugs down the toilet?

— No.

I checked the ashy trail my hit had left on the foil. It looked like half a swastika.

— Give me another nub, then don't give me anymore no matter what I say.

— You need to call your sponsor.

— He's in Cuba.

And then, just like that, the dope wanting peels away and my poor little junk-stained brain makes a possible connection. It's not a sure thing, but it's something.

— Go ahead, smoke your crack, we got a few hours to kill.

He heads for the bathroom like a furloughed soldier on his way to a ten-dollar whore.

— Hold on, give me that nub.

37.

It's 6:55 in the morning and I'm staring at a framed black-and-white poster of Martin Luther King, Malcolm X, and Barack Obama. A mandatory artifact in every living room in South Central L.A. It used to just be Marty and Malcolm and in certain feistier homes, Marcus Garvey, but old Barack went and grabbed the big prize, so now he's the father, son, or holy ghost, depending on how you look at it.

— Let me hold the key.

— Why?

— Because, I don't want you jumping in an Uber and disappearing with it.

We're at Robert Lee's. Kyle's sitting on the fake suede couch with the plastic slip covers, and I'm in the baby-shit-colored recliner with the duct tape X over the rip in the arm.

— Ain't even seven o'clock.

That's Bob muttering from the other room. He had come to the door looking like a black Methuselah, his old, ashy knees poking out through a junkie bathrobe. But now he's got his dad jeans on, as he comes out pulling sleep debris from his dented 'fro.

— You two done made up, huh?

— You call him?

— Yeah, but it went right to self-pick-up. That fool can't keep his phone on more than a week.

— He's not answering or it's off?

— Think it off. You know how he be, Bow-Be. He call you when he need you, but when you need him you got to go find his ass.

I didn't feel myself go into the nod, but I felt myself come out of it. When I did, Robert Lee was staring at me, his nose all scrunched up like he smelled something putrid.

— You done fucked up, ain't you? Why you go and do that, Bow-Be?

— I'm not high. I just haven't slept.

— Don't fucking lie to him, you relapsed, admit it.

Kyle just can't resist the opportunity to let Robert Lee know he's not the biggest fuckup in the room. I look up at Robert Lee like he's my dad.

— I just smoked a couple of hits. I'm not going to get strung out again.

— I don't care. You want to get back in the game, that's your business, son. You just been doing so good.

— I'll be okay.

We both know I probably won't.

— Well shit, let me go take care of my thing then, I was rushin' for y'all.

— No, let's just go.

— Let him do his wake-up.

Kyle again. Now he's an advocate for junkie rights.

— You know where he is?

— He either over where he stay at or at Momma's.

— *Momma*, momma?

— Yeah. Ain't but one Momma. He go over there sometime, got a little trick stay 'round the corner.

— Well, let's swing by his place and Momma's quick and if he ain't there you come back and do your thing.

— Why you need to talk to Captain so bad, Bow-Be?

I was ready for Kyle to pop off again, but luckily, he kept his mouth shut.

— Tell you later, it's too much to get into right now.

— You come knock on my door this early, now you ain't even want to tell me what's going on?

— Robert Lee, I'd tell you, but *I* don't even really know.

— You know enough you ready to go by Momma's house seven in the morning. And you done messed around.

— That ain't got nothing to do with it.

— That always got something to do it. You ain't thinking straight.

— Let's just wait 'til later.

That's Kyle. I spin on him.

— Dude, *shut up*, let me handle this, all right?

— Handle what? What you handlin' son?

— Robert Lee. I just need to talk to Captain.

He looks at me like I have no idea how the world really works. It's a look I haven't seen for a while.

— It's just a little detail having to do with Carla.

He takes another sniff of something bad, then turns to Kyle.

— This about the girl?

Kyle's not sure what to say, so he says, "Yeah."

— Don't you get me caught up in nothing to do with that girl.

— You're not going to get caught up in anything.

Now I'm scuffling just to hold my ground.

— Not Captain neither, come on Bow-Be, you know better than that.

— Robert Lee, stop, it's not like that.

I catch a heavy whiff of old soup, which is the default smell of Bob's apartment.

— Captain's got nothing to do with this, he just might have an address I need.

— Whose address?

— Robert Lee, man, why you asking so many questions?

He stares at me like I'm a stranger.

— What's going on, Bow-Be?

— I thought you didn't want to be involved?

— I don't.

— Then trust me to know how to handle my business.

It's a hell of a thing for a Jewish screenwriter from Long Island to say to an old black junkie.

— I trust you Bow-Be, I just don't trust whatever you up to.

— I'm not up to anything.

— Then why you here so early? You ain't sick.

He's right, I'm not, but I'm not high anymore either.

— Just go do your thing. Seriously man, get yourself straight, then we'll figure this shit out. Go ahead, you're right, I'm not in that big a rush.

I add a little chuckle at the end to make it clear that this is all a misunderstanding and it's no big deal, but I can tell from Bob's look it's too late for that. But he doesn't pass on the chance to do his wake-up.

— I ain't gonna be long.

He heads for the bedroom, calling back.

— But I ain't having nothing to do with nothing having to do with that girl.

#

It's been half an hour and Robert Lee's still in the bedroom. Between the soup smell and the old Vaseline carpet I've had to step outside twice and grab some air. Ten minutes in, Kyle decided he was tired of Bob's struggle, so he stepped into the bathroom to see if he could get it right. He did, and quickly. Now, he's smacked back in the recliner like Charlie Parker on payday.

I take a seat on the arm of the slipcover couch and consider my situation. A week ago, I was a car, a meager and ridiculous car, but a car, and I could go wherever I wanted. But now I've become a train, a mindless, unstoppable train and I can only go where the tracks lead me. Kyle's doubled over in the big chair like a ventriloquist's dummy without a hand up his back. And that's when it grabs my eye, the light through the window catching it with a white glint. I slowly push myself to standing and see if Kyle stirs.

He doesn't. He's nodding, not sleeping, so he could come out of it at any moment, whether there's noise or not. If I was a good thief, I would just walk over to him and take the chain casually, but I'm not, so I tiptoe the five steps, my heart like a kick drum. I stand over him, looking down at his folded body and the bare nape of his neck. I reach down carefully to where the chain hangs free from under his chin, but before I can take it he falls over to one side, his body hanging over the recliner's edge. He's even higher than he was at Big Boy.

I move over to the side of the chair and sit down on the floor in front of him. His head is six inches off the carpet. I reach for the chain and begin to slowly lift it off his neck. I'm halfway home when I feel a heat. I look up and there's Robert Lee, standing in his bedroom door, his eyes full of pity. Finally, he closes the door, and leaves me to my business. I get the chain off Kyle's neck, take a last glance at the three wise men on the wall and am out the door with the key clutched in my hand.

38.

The house looks like it was just placed there. Not built from the ground up but set down with a giant hand like a toy. This is Momma's place, a small little clapboard shack on Jefferson just east of Western. I would have gone over to Captain's spot first, but I was only there once and all I remember is that it was a back house behind a place you could barely call a front house. But Momma's house I know, though I haven't been there in fifteen years.

I stash my car at the Food 4 Less parking lot across Western and stand on the corner waiting for the light. The Guatemalans are all on their way to work. I make eye contact with the little Mayan granny selling Styrofoam cups of that sweet cinnamon rice porridge Central Americans eat in the morning. Strangers look at you different when you got a black eye.

I get across Western and turn up Momma's front walk. The grass is uncut and there's an old Pontiac on cinder blocks in the driveway, half its ass showing under a crumpled blue tarp. I ring the bell 'cause I figure the cops would knock and I don't want to scare the shit out of anyone, or worse, get myself shot. If it was 1998 she'd come to door and I'd say "Hey Momma" and she'd say, "Hey baby," but it's not 1998, it's right fucking now, and when the door finally opens she's not standing there, a dude is. A dude I recognize. A dude I was hoping I'd never see again.

— Who you?

Does he really not know who I am?

— Hey man. Is Momma home?

— Yeah, she here. What you want with her?

What the fuck was I thinking coming over here without Robert Lee?

— Just wanted to say hello, I'm an old friend.

He quickly scans the street like any reasonable gangster would with a stranger at his door.

— Kinda early for a visit.

— I know, sorry. I was in the neighborhood.

He's in a black nylon wife-beater and unbuttoned jeans. He must be in his mid-forties now, but he's still tight and coiled with a "borderline" gleam in his eye.

— How you know Momma?

— Just from around. I was part of the after-clinic breakfast crowd back in the day.

He doesn't love that answer, but he doesn't hate it either.

— Who I say is here?

I can't decide whether to give a fake name or to just ask for Captain and keep Momma out it.

— Edmond ... It's me ... Bobby.

The name means nothing to him, and neither does my face.

— Uncle Kenny's friend.

Now he gets it. His eyes narrow.

— What you doing here?

Edmond is Kenny Butler's nephew and the last time I'd seen him, he had pulled a knife on me. He was pissed because I told Kenny I thought it was him who had stolen my brand-new laptop out of the trunk of my car. Actually, I knew it was him because Kenny's brother Jay saw him do it, but I guess Edmond thought I should have just kept my mouth shut and taken it as some kind of white-boy tax for doing business in the hood. Luckily, he knew Kenny would be real pissed if he took it past a threat, but he was more than capable. He had already stabbed every adult who lived in that house except Kenny, and they all had the same belly scar to prove it.

— I just want to say hello to Momma for a minute.

— She ain't sell no pills no more, she damn near ninety.

— I don't want pills. Look, you know Robert Lee, old pardner of your uncle's lives over on 39th and Budlong.

— What about him?

— Well, I'm looking for Captain. Robert Lee say sometimes he stays over here.

He looks at me like he doesn't believe a word I'm saying.

— Robert Lee sent you over here?

— No, he just told me Captain might be here.

He pushes up the wife-beater and scratches the black wisps on his yellow cobra belly.

— He here, but he sleepin'.

— Can I talk to him?

— He ain't gonna wake up for you. He been drinkin'.

— Can I try?

He waits a long beat before he answers, looking down on me from the top of his 6'2" tower.

— I didn't take your shit, understand? I wasn't even there that day.

It's twenty-five years and neither one of us has forgotten.

— Cool, man. I believe you.

I say it as a peace offering, but it makes him hate me even more. He points with a long-nailed finger like he's banishing me to oblivion.

— End of the fuckin' hall.

#

I knock with a loud pop. It's a front door knock, but I already tried it bedroom-style ten times and all I got was crickets. I put my ear to the door hoping for a sign of life. Nothing. Fuck it! I just turn the knob and poke my head in. The first thing I see is a short black wig lying on the floor like a dead rabbit. A few feet past that, a pair of greasy blue work pants and a pile of tiger-stripe lycra. Just beyond that is a bottle of cheap brandy, lying on its side, and behind all of it, a stained and half-stripped mattress with two bodies in it. I'm hoping one of them is Captain.

— Captain ... Captain ... Captain?

I increase the volume each time, but it's having the same effect as the knocks.

— Yo Captain.

Nothing. I push through the door and take a few steps into the room.

— Yo, Captain, wake up.

The room's small and in three strides I'm on top of them. Them being Captain and a half-covered, near-bald black woman with a big fatty tit wedged under her side.

— Captain!

He doesn't stir, but she does with a start.

— Who the fuck is you!

— Hey, sorry. I just need to talk to Captain.

I try to say it like it's no big deal, but it doesn't play in Peoria.

— Get your ass the fuck out of here!

She scrambles for a torn sheet and pulls it over her.

— Look, it's okay, I'm an old friend of his. Edmond let me in.

— Where my purse? Where my motherfuckin' purse?!

I spot her bag on the floor and hand it to her as a peace offering.

— Here ... I'm really sorry, Edmond didn't tell me Captain had someone in here with him.

— You just don't *come* into a room where *I'm* sleepin'!

— I'm sorry, I'm an old friend of Robert Lee, you know Robert Lee?

I'm trying to show her that I'm a member of the team and know the players, but she's more interested in what's in the bag. When her hand comes out holding a pistol, I understand why.

— Now you *get* your ass out this room or I will put a bullet in your *fuckin'* head!

It's the first time I've ever had a gun pointed at me, and my first thought is, this is it! I'm going to die now.

— I will shoot you, understand me? I will shoot you dead.

I look at the small black gun and the bulging eyes behind it and just start pleading.

— Please, just put the gun down. I'm going.

— What's your name?

— You'll never see me again, I promise.

I begin to back out of the room.

— I said, what's your fuckin' name?!

— Bobby.

— What the fuck you doin' bitch? Put that burner down.

It's Captain, at least this woke him up. She keeps the gun on me but talks to him.

— You know this fuckin' white boy?

Captain turns and looks at me. He's half asleep, and hung over.

— Yeah, I know him. What you doing here, Bobby? What time is it?

But my eyes are still on the lady with the gun.

— I'm sorry, I didn't mean to scare you, I didn't know you were in here.

— You didn't *scare* me motherfucker, you just *surprised* my ass!

Captain is leaning off the bed looking at a watch on the floor.

— Ain't even eight o'clock. What you doin' over here so early Bobby, you sick?

— No. I'm not sick.

— Who tell you I was over here? Robert Lee?

— Yeah.

— Shit. Well, what you need?

— I just need to talk to you.

— 'Bout what?

I don't want to talk in front of Captain's friend, but I don't want to offend her either.

— You can talk in front of Teeny, she cool.

She's anything but cool, but I don't have much choice.

— Captain, you remember the other day when we were talking out in front of Robert Lee's.

— Yeah, don't tell me you come over here this early for that ten dollars?

— No, that's yours. But remember we were talkin' about that girl, you know, Carla.

— The dead girl. What about her?

— You said she asked you to fix a motorcycle.

— Yeah, old Triumph cafe racer.

— And you said you went to meet her, but she never showed.

— Nope. Didn't even call or nothing.

— You remember where you were going to meet her?

— Yeah. Storage space where she keep the bike.

Jackpot!

— You remember where that was?

— Hell yeah.

— She tell you which space, the number?

— Yeah, she wrote it all down.

Now it's time to ask the $64,000-dollar question.

— Captain, is there any possible chance you still have it?

He laughs like I just told a joke.

— Hell no.

The air goes out of my lungs.

— I ain't have to keep it. I remembered it soon as I saw it.

— You remember the number?

— Uh-huh.

— Don't you tell him, Captain, you make him pay for that.

That's Teeny. She whips her head to me.

— You want that number, you need to pay this man.

— Be quiet Teeny, Bobby an old pardner of mine.

He swings up and sits on the bed with his feet on the floor.

— What you want with that bike, Bobby?

— I don't want the bike. I just need to know which storage space.

— Don't you tell him, Captain. That man need to pay you.

— You need to stop, girl.

— He need to pay you. You know he do.

— Captain, it's cool. I can give you some money.

— He want a thousand dollars.

Now she's Captain's agent.

— I can't give him a thousand dollars.

— Then he ain't tellin' you shit.

— Will you shut the fuck up and stay out of my damn business. Damn.

Captain rubs some sleep from his eyes, then hops over to the brandy in his boxer shorts. He takes it back to the bed and tilts the bottle back, so he can get the dregs. I'm still jelly legged and mouth dry from having a gun pointed at me.

— So why you need this bike?

— I told you, I don't need the bike. I just need the number and location of the storage space.

— Why he want it? Make him tell you Captain.

— Hush, girl.

— No, this man come over here like that this early in the morning, he want that information for a *reason*. And he need to *pay* for that information. That information worth five hundred dollars at least.

— I don't have five hundred dollars.

— Well, you better go find it, 'cause you want that number, *somebody* gonna have to come up with five hundred dollars.

— How 'bout the motorcycle. You want the motorcycle?

— I don't want no stolen motorcycle. Shit, I'm too old go back to prison. How much money you got on you, Bobby?

— Not a lot.

— He lyin', check his pockets.

— Can you part with a couple hundred?

— All I got is a couple of hundred, Captain. But you can have half of it.

— Don't you take no hundred dollars.

Captain looks at the near empty bottle.

— Aright, that sound okay.

— You a fool, Captain. That man ready to give you a thousand dollars.

— How much you wake up with Teeny?

She answers with an acne scowl.

— If I told you a man gonna walk in here this morning and give you a hundred dollars is you gonna say "no"?

— That man ready to give you more than a hundred dollars.

— I told you Bobby an old pardner of mine. I know you ain't gonna be turnin' down the dope I buy with that money.

He turns back to me with his own scowl and puts some extra mustache in it.

— Just gimme the hundred, shit.

I reach into my pocket and pull out what I hope is five twenties. It turns out to be a few more.

— You sure you remember the number?

— Hell yeah. 4-16. I couldn't forget that, that's my momma's birthday.

— Your momma an Aries? That explain a lot.

That's Teeny again. She pulls the bottle from Captain and knocks off the last dribble. I put the money in his now empty hand.

— Take a hundred forty dollars.

— Thanks, Bobby.

— Which storage place?

— That one up on Santa Monica and Highland. Up around you.

— I know it. Okay, I'm gonna take off.

I tip my chin up to Teeny.

— Nice to meet you.

Teeny mumbles something back but it's not quite words.

As for Captain, he just seems happy to have his morning's issue squared away. By the time he calls "Hey Bobby, who give you that black eye?" I'm halfway down the hall.

39.

Trejo's Coffee & Donuts is a Pepto-Bismol-colored bunker with Danny Trejo's trademark tough hombre portrait plastered across the side. It's catty-corner to Public Storage, which I'm gazing at out the window like it's a pretty girl I'm scared to ask to dance. I'm feeling empty, so I buy an apple fritter which I destroy in four savage bites. I try to get some too-hot coffee down to fight off the junk haze but burn my mouth instead. I know I'm supposed to be the hunter, but it feels I'm the one on the run. The only thing I know for sure is that I've crossed the line. Fuck crossed it, I've eviscerated it. If I had an ounce of sense I'd run out of here, get my ass to an AA meeting, raise my hand and say, "I relapsed. I have heroin in my glove compartment. Take me to rehab now!"

I put the coffee down on the counter, close my eyes, and take a deep breath through my nose. That's better. And then, with no warning, a huge acidic bullfrog of fried dough and coffee leaps up out of my gut and blasts out my mouth, as I lunge for the trash can. There's some on the floor, some on the window and some on the can, but none *in* it. The tatted punk-rock hipster chick behind the counter shrieks "What the fuck, dude!" I raise my hand, half in apology, half in surrender, and stumble out the door.

#

I'm just up the block from Public Storage and I have absolutely no idea what to do. The place looks impenetrable. A four-story prison for unwanted dressers. I have a faint memory of renting a space from them under dire circumstances, and that there's some kind of access code involved. I could go back down to see if Captain knows that as well, but it's probably longer than his mother's birthday. Maybe it's her Social Security number. I'm pretty sure lingering up the street like a pedophile at a schoolyard isn't helping my cause, but this part of Citrus Avenue is weird as shit to begin with, sidewalk on one side only, and the plainclothes façades of post-production houses filling out the block.

I take out my device and try googling "how to get into Public Storage without an access code." All I find is a story about a couple who got trapped inside after-hours and had to call the fire department to get out. I could go to the office and say, "Look, I've just destroyed what little was left of my life acquiring the key to a storage space which was rented from you by a tragic but compelling woman who died a few weeks ago in a crack motel taking the access code with her. I didn't know her well, but I dated her sister for a bit and she asked me to track down an old friend which led to all kinds of nonsense that you don't really need to know, but the basic takeaway is, I really got to get into her storage space, so what do you say?"

The wind whips down the block with post-apocalyptic glee. After the bomb drops, there will only be cockroaches and color correction. Fuck it, when in doubt, play it straight. I'm just going to go in there and find out what it takes to open a storage space that belongs to a dead person.

I cross the street and walk into the building's gaping garage door of a mouth. It's more of a parking structure than it is an office building. To the left are double glass doors, uniformed employees behind counters like at FedEx or the airport, the horrible lab-rat glare of fluorescent light. Straight ahead, a big orange drive-through prison gate protecting America's stuff. A white Volkswagen Golf rolls by on my right and up to it. Out comes a female hand. It taps at a touch-tone pad. I decide not to turn for the office but keep walking straight.

My heart's beating fast and shallow. I'm close enough to see the tapping hand has yellow nail polish. The gate starts moving with a grinding hum, as the hand returns to the car. The gate slowly disappears and the car rolls through. I decide to go for it and walk in right behind. I wait for someone to shout, "Stop that guy!" but they don't. I hear the gate closing behind me as I move past two Latino dudes with bright orange paint on long rollers. They nod at me, I nod back. To my left and right are storage spaces, all with numbers. I reach a wide-doored elevator and hit the button. The door opens. I get in.

#

Storage Space #416 looks like all the others, a bright orange corrugated metal door with a round company-issued padlock. There's cameras all over, so I try to act like I belong there, meaning

STRAIGHT DOPE   **177**

I sort of slump and yawn, as I lift the chain from around my neck
and take the small key in hand. I'm convinced there's no way this
can work, as I am convinced about everything in my life, but the
key slides in with a click, and turns easily. The lock pops open. Don't
ever doubt a black man's word when it comes to his mother.

I raise the corrugated metal door with a rumble, flip on the light
and am confronted with a total clusterfuck: boxes, milk crates,
plastic storage tubs, dark garbage bags with torn skin and
distended bellies, all of it looking like it was tossed from a speeding
truck. Front and center are a couple of armless mannequins with
pink wigs, red lipstick and painted black pubic hair. Two others lay
horizontal on a storage tub, on top of each other like they're fucking.
There's some old standing lamps, an expensive-looking green
leather sofa and a beautiful blonde wood coffee table piled on it
topside down. Next to that, an antique steamer trunk covered in
old baggage stickers: Hotel Strand, Rangoon Burma. Hotel Zeben,
Den Haag Holland. Hotel Imperial, Shanghai, Manager Chen Yu
Shen. Probably grandma's, or maybe it just caught Carla's eye at
some Sotheby's auction and Otto bid on them to keep her awake.

On top of the trunk sits a little clump of books that I recognize
immediately. It's The "Big Book" of Alcoholics Anonymous, the gold
and green NA workbook, the 12 & 12 (*Twelve Steps and Twelve
Traditions*) and a copy of *One Day at a Time*. It's the set that's
waiting in your room when you check into rehab.

I clock a plastic laundry basket filled with abandoned vegetable
juicers and their mismatched attachments. Rich girl purchases for
those short-lived stabs at health between dope runs. Against the
back wall are the books. If you check the binders I'm sure you'll find
Burroughs, Baudelaire, Poe, Coleridge, Hubert Selby. All the usual
suspects, all the patron saints of smack. Everything in here is a
clue. The forensic evidence of a life put on hold. Junk demands you
travel light. Just a bag, a spoon, a rig, a pack of smokes, a source
of cash and a lighter. You can't be weighed down by a Hans Wegner
"shell chair" when you're moving at dope speed. You don't need your
original Jules and Jim poster when the only wall you have to
hang it on is down at the Snooty Fox.

My eye gets pulled to the old Triumph cafe racer, which leans
against the wall. It's badass and innocent just like the century it
comes from. But it's what's next to it that really gets my attention.
A long, stainless steel clothes rack with lots of dry cleaning still in

the plastic. Interspersed between are garment bags from Saks, Barney's, Armani. Seems as good a place to start as any.

#

Nothing! I unzip every goddamn one of those bags, but all I find are clothes. Fancy clothes. Mostly coats. Beautiful cashmere and camel hair coats. Coats some rich dude buys you for five grand, but you end up selling for $300 on your way to the 'hood.

Fuck. Now what? There's too much shit to go through. I start just tearing through shit like a badger on adderol when I get a text. It's from Kyle. Two simple, heartfelt words. "NOT COOL".

#

I'm digging through bags and boxes, unearthing the artifacts of a life cut short when I come across an item of interest. It's an old, worn brown leather bag. I remember Otto calling the bag Carla left with a "valise" and this is about as valisey as it gets. But when I get it open, I don't find the robe. I find a large, zippered, black portfolio, the kind giraffe-thin models used to tote around New York City back in the day. It makes total sense that a girl like Carla would have a modeling book, and I figure it's full of pictures of her at seventeen, bright-eyed, innocent, and ready to conquer the world. I'm way off.

The first one is an action shot. Carla from the waist up in a black tuxedo jacket, her hands pulling apart the lapels like she's flashing someone on a bus. Her head is flung to the side with long hair flying, and the mouth is in profile with a ball gag in it. Above her bare, fist-sized breasts, written in red lipstick is the word "ART." The picture has a fierce gravity, and sucks me in like a black hole. My eyes fly around the photo but keep returning to the blood red brand on her chest. It's strong personal politics. You can't objectify me because I'm objectifying myself.

I turn the big, plastic-sleeved page and there she is again, shot low from the side wearing nothing but a strap-on cow-milking stool. The stool has a belted harness, a tiny swing seat and one stainless steel leg with a wide spring at the bottom like a pogo stick. It's hardcore agricultural kink, the single leg a mechanical cock, except it's coming out of her ass, not going in. The second I see it I know I'll never get the image out of my head. This photo has no feminist overtones, it's just fucking twisted.

And then, as if I haven't been scarred enough already, the next pic just blows the back of my head off. It's tight on her incredible face, the eyes sad and searching and her lipstick slut-smeared across her aching mouth. It goes into my brain like a hot spike. The pleading in the eyes, the crazy innocence of her freckles set against the battered mouth. It's so ruthless and intimate it makes me think I really did know her. I can't stay there with her so I keep flipping pages: She's bent over a table with one torn stocking. She's bare-assed in red Chuck Taylors and a dog leash, striping her back. She's naked in a chair reading Nietzsche, a cup of steaming coffee between her open legs. She's doubled over laughing wearing a trucker cap and a blue strap-on. She's sitting at a kitchen table naked with a needle in her arm, high and heartbroken as Billie Holiday.

Some of these shots are hot, some are playful, some are lurid, but all of them are sad. It's like a sacrifice, and the only suitable ending would be a shot of her getting thrown into a volcano by an Aztec priest.

I close the book and put it back in the bag. What kind of world is this? The most incredible, tender, mysterious girl I ever met was a junkie and a pervert and I end up involved with her uptight Al-Anon sister. And then I look over to my left and I know.

40.

One of my favorite movies is *It's a Mad Mad Mad Mad World*. A three-hour and twenty-five-minute epic comedy made in 1963 by Stanley Kramer. The movie begins with a car frantically passing other cars on a winding mountain road until it sails off a cliff, soars through the air and crashes on the rocks below. Sid Caesar, Milton Berle, Buddy Hackett, Mickey Rooney and Jonathan Winters rush down to the accident site to find Jimmy Durante lying near death. He tells them, "There's money, a lot of it, 350 Gs worth, and it's buried under a big W ... A big W, I tell ya." Well, those two mannequins fucking are my Big W, and it was Carla's pictures that made the bell go off.

I go over and yank the top one off, with no respect for their intimacy. Then I get rid of the bottom, so I can get to the red plastic tub underneath. I take the lid off. There's flat brown cardboard on top, and under that a gray plastic tarp. Is it an art stash, or a chopped-up body? I get rid of the tarp and find a good-sized black Adidas duffle bag. I pull it out, put it on the sofa and go for the zipper. The first thing I find are three small Bubble Wrap-covered rectangles. I figure they're the Hockney fakes, but I don't even care, I'm focused on what's underneath. It's a clear plastic garment bag folded over and stuffed with what looks like gauze or cheesecloth. I unzip it and lay whatever's wrapped in the cheesecloth gently on the sofa. I unwrap it carefully, layer by layer until I see it. A one-foot square of shiny gold fabric. Matisse is in the house.

I rewrap the package and put it back in the bag. I grab the portfolio with Carla's photos, and throw it in along with the fake Hockneys. There's a third package in there as well. It's large and wrapped in so much worn silver duct tape it looks like the mummified remains of a quadruple amputee. I know it's the "something else" Otto spoke of, but I'm too gakked up to even think about dealing with it now. But I'm *not* too gakked to notice a business card cradled in the duffle's bottom. The card is pale green and says, "Tenth Muse Gallery." It's got a Santa Monica address. At first, I don't give it much thought, and just zip the duffle closed, but then I start mulling things over in my head. And the more I mull, the sicker I get. But this time it has nothing to do with dope.

41.

I walk across the open plaza and sit down on a bench in front of something called The Lynda and Stewart Resnick Pavilion. Jews love to put their name on shit: buildings, scholarships, corned beef sandwiches. If it'll be seen in public, some fancy Jew will pay to have his name on it.

I'm at LACMA, and the midday museum crowd is getting their art on. Sleeveless, teenage cuties are taking selfies in front of something called "Urban Light," an installation of 30s L.A. streetlamps that grows near the edge of Wilshire like a stand of iron corn. Across from me folks wolf down lunch at some mid-century-themed clip joint, famished after three hours of mandatory culture. Museums are weird, I go to 'em 'cause that's where they keep the good shit, but it's been my experience that the best art shows up when you're not looking for it.

I see a really great looking well-put-together woman wander in from the 6th Street side and get a little buzz from the way she moves through space. Then I realize it's her. Guess she didn't lose her looks in the last twenty-four hours. She stops and searches around for me, wearing big sunglasses and a white straw fedora. She looks almost as good in her hat as I do in mine. Now she's turning in circles like a lost child at the fair. Finally, she spots me and makes her way over. I stand and give her a hug, the kind you give to an ex it didn't end well with.

— Copping my personal style, huh?

— You mean the hat. You've seen this before, haven't you?

— I don't think so. Very classy. But with just enough whimsy to get the job done.

She sits down, puts her bag to the side and crosses her legs like she's done it before. The rose perfume's still in my nose from the hug, but I'm not going down that road.

— I haven't been here in the longest. The last time may have been the Caravaggio.

— I saw that. Lot of energy coming out of *those* canvases.

— He's something else entirely.

— Entirely.

— Are you making fun of me?

— Always.

Normally it would have been "are you making fun of me, sweetie" but after that fucked-up scene with Liam at the W she had enough sense to keep it formal.

— So, what made you want to meet here?

— I don't know. It's on theme and somewhere between us. And it's out in the open.

— Out in the open? That's a peculiar thing to say. Are you concerned for your safety?

— Not yet. But you just got here.

She sniffed a laugh and looked out straight ahead, or at least I think she did. The giant five-hundred-dollar sunglasses kept it a mystery.

— I'm sorry.

— For what, me being attracted to you?

— For all of it. For being such a troublemaker back when we first met.

— You couldn't help yourself. Addicts don't know what to do with genuine affection.

I had set her up to say, "I'm sorry too" and start explaining about the other day, but she didn't know enough to let the writer guide the scene. She stopped gazing at the lunch crowd and put the big Chanel peepers on me.

— Have you slept? You look like New Year's Day in Amsterdam.

— It's just the black eye.

— The other's darker than that one. I can't tell which is which! She pressed down her skirt like she was about to stand.

— I have to be somewhere soon.

— Oh yeah, where?

— Bobby, please, you know I'm very fond of you, and I was horrified about the way Liam behaved the other day, but if this was going to work between you and me, it would have worked already, so let's just leave it as it is, shall we?

— I saw Otto Schlein last night.

The words stopped her dead and she lost ten pounds on the spot.

— When was the last time you saw Carla?

She didn't answer.

— Take your glasses off.

— It's too bright.

— Take your glasses off. I want to see your face when you talk.

It took a moment, but the glasses came off revealing a pair of scared blue eyes.

— When was the last time you saw her?

— He called you directly or had Liam do it?

— He called me, and we met for a drink.

— You don't drink.

— I do now. Tell me about Carla.

She looked down into her lap.

— When you don't look at me I think you're lying.

— Please, Bobby, let's just go to my car.

— Why, is that where your gun is?

— Have you lost your mind?

— I sure fucking have. Tell me about Carla.

— I can't remember. It was either her last stay at Friendly House or I think we may have had lunch after that in Santa Monica.

— Did she come by the gallery?

— No. We just met for lunch. What did Otto say to you?

— That was the last time you saw her?

— Yes.

— I don't believe you.

— I don't care what you believe. What did Otto want to talk to you about?

— You don't know?

— No.

I didn't want to believe her, but the way she said "no" made me know it was true.

— He wants to talk to Kyle, in person. He has a surveillance tape of Carla leaving his place with the robe and getting into a car, and he thinks Kyle was driving.

The eyes got blue with relief.

— But he wasn't. You were.

— That's absurd!

It came out two octaves higher than everything before it.

— Who said that, did Kyle tell you that? You're going to believe the word of a drug addict and a murderer.

— He didn't kill her.

— How do you know?!

She was getting shrieky and a couple of young Korean kids stopped to stare. The parents scooped them up with a wave and a "sorry." I turned back to Angie and lowered my voice.

— Look, I don't know what's going on with you, or why you haven't told me one honest word since I came to your house, but I was ninety percent sure you were driving that car when I got here, and I'm one hundred percent sure now. Now, I don't know why I called you, and I'm probably going to regret doing it, but for some reason I have some actual feeling for your bizarre English ass, so if I were you, I would start telling me the fucking truth.

— And why should I do that?

— Because I've got the bag with the art.

42.

— What is that?

— I don't know.

— You've never seen it before?

— No. Where's the smock?

— I've got the smock. I want to know about this.

We're staring down at the duct tape mummy lying in the middle of a lumpy bed.

— Did Carla mention it?

— No, she got in the car with the bag, and I dropped her at some apartment in Hollywood. We had a plan to meet the next day, but she never showed.

She looks around the dark little room with its filthy carpet and wall-bolted TV.

— Do we have to be here? This room is absolutely ghastly.

We're in a tiny cell at the Starlight Motel on Washington near La Brea, an L-shaped row of forty-dollar stalls that border a potholed gash of bumpy driveway. I brought her here because I was tired of the tea selection at the W and because Kyle or Grygor or God knows who might be hanging around my place, but most of all 'cause it was the seventh game and I wanted to be on my home court.

— Do you think she knew this was in the bag when she took it?

— I don't know.

— Did she mention the Hockneys to you?

— No, but Liam did.

— Otto says they're fakes.

— I'm not surprised. He often has forgeries he sells to arms dealers and human trafficker types.

She put her hand to her head like she was getting a migraine.

— The smell in this room is starting to make me physically ill; please, Bobby, I don't excuse how I've behaved, but this is abuse.

— Stop being so dramatic. I need to find out what this fucking thing is.

— Then hurry up and open it.

— I'm not sure I should.

— Well, how else are we going to find out what's inside?

— Maybe I shouldn't find out. Maybe I should just bring it back to him.

I look at the duct tape lump. It's as creepy and nefarious a package as I've ever seen in my life.

— Fuck, I don't know what to do.

— What did he ask you to do?

— He asked me to get him in a room with Kyle. I should just bring the dude his shit back and get my money.

— How much?

— He didn't say. He just said he'd put some marks in my pocket.

— That's very Otto.

I fall down into a chair, as a big breaker of overwhelm comes crashing down on my head. I glance up at Angie, looking for some softness.

— I relapsed.

I don't know if I want sympathy, rescuing or I just want her to feel guilty for getting me into all this shit.

— What? When?

— Last night.

— Oh my God, Bobby, are you okay?

— I don't fucking know. I don't fucking know anything.

Now I'm being dramatic, but she bites on it, and comes and put her hand on my shoulder.

— I know you must be devastated, but can we just get out of this room, so we can think sane thoughts?

I push up out of the chair, and go over to the duct tape lump. Fuck it.

#

— Be careful, Bobby, you don't want to cut what's inside.

I'm holding the black rubber grips on a long pair of red bolt cutters, the kind they use to snip the padlock off your locker when you don't pay your dues at the Y. I had gone to the front desk and gotten a pair of scissors, but that was like trying to bring down an elephant with a BB gun, so I went back and asked the desk guy if he had anything stronger. He disappeared and came back with the big bolt cutters, and said "Here, these good for handcuffs."

— It's like cutting fucking cement. They must have used ten rolls on this thing.

I've only made it about six inches across the package and my hands are already killing me.

— Come here and pull while I cut.

She came and put her hands on the package.

— You sure you don't have any idea what's in here?

— No, but I'm getting an eerie feeling.

With her stretching the slit I started to make some real progress, and soon there were only a couple of inches left.

— Okay, that's enough. Go on, take it out.

— No, you do it.

— You do it, you're the art expert.

She looks at the mummy, then goes to her bag, removes a stainless-steel water bottle, unscrews the cap, and takes a gulp.

— You all right?

— I've just been overcome with the strangest sensation. Like a blade up the spine.

— Drink some more water.

— It's passing. Please, Bobby, you do it.

I lay the big bolt cutters on the bed and dig my hands into the duct tape tomb. Inside is a large lump of wrapped black plastic like a great big loaf of bread. It's taped at the edges, but I've had my fill of tape, so I just tear at the middle.

— No, don't!

But it's too late. I reach inside the torn plastic and remove a hunk of rolled canvas. I start unrolling.

— Don't do that, it could be extremely old or delicate. We need to take it somewhere clean and do this correctly.

I keep unrolling, but more slowly and carefully.

— I'm trembling. My body is physically trembling.

Her voice is calm, but the eyes are on fire.

We're looking down at a painted canvas, maybe five feet by three feet. A ghostly image of a young, dark-haired woman in a high-necked, long-sleeved white dress. She's standing with her arms unnaturally, but not stiffly at her sides. The dress is soft-focus and impressionistic, but the face feels like a photograph, the mouth a dark, sensuous red even though the painting is black and white. It's an act of magic and the whole canvas radiates with a brutal innocence, both tragic and hopeful at once.

— Do you know what you're looking at?

— No.

— Check the signature.

I look down in the right-hand corner. In large, crude stick figure letters are two words, one on top of the other. "Gustav" and "Klimt".
— Gustav Klimt.
— You know him of course?
— Yeah. I know who he is. Klimt. I'm not super familiar with his work, but I know him. He's German, right?
— Austrian. This is a very famous painting, Bobby. The portrait of Trude Steiner. It's one of the most important missing pieces of World War II. I wrote a paper on plundered Nazi art in school and this piece figured in it prominently. I'm having a bit of an out-of-body experience.
— Are you sure it's real? I mean, he deals in fakes, right?
— That's no forgery, trust me. Of course, it has to be authenticated, but you can take me out of here feet first if that isn't the real *Bildnis Trude Steiner*.

I didn't know what "bildnis" meant but the super-German way she said it made things even more intense than they already were.
— What's it worth?
— You can't put a price on it. It's the missing Klimt. The entire world has been searching for this painting for nearly a century.
— What do you think he's going to do with it?
— Otto? I don't know, it's not easy to sell. Even if he came upon it legitimately, which I know he didn't, the original family has a claim on it.

She looks back down at it with a wonder normally reserved for mothers and their newborns.
— *Bildnis Trude Steiner*. My God Bobby, I have to think.
— There's nothing to think about, I'm bringing it back it to him.
— Why? Does he know you have it?
— No, he doesn't know I have any of this shit.
— Then let's just hold on for a moment. I don't think you understand how important this piece is.
— I don't care, I'm not getting killed over it.
— Oh, please, Bobby, this isn't one of your scripts. Nobody's getting killed. And besides, Otto's not a killer.
— It's not Otto I'm worried about, it's the other guys.
— What other guys?
— He said there were other people and that they didn't give a shit about Kyle or Carla, so they sure as hell aren't going to give a shit about me. Besides I already had a gun pointed at me earlier this

morning, I'm fucking done.

— Will you please just calm down. Is this the drugs talking?

— Yeah, it's the drugs. If I was straight, I'd be super relaxed about driving around with a stolen one-hundred-million-dollar painting the whole world is looking for in the trunk of my Toyota.

— My God, aren't you even a little awed to find yourself in the presence of a missing masterpiece?

— No. Not at the moment. Right now, it's just one more thing freaking me out.

I get hit by a wave of nausea and head for the bathroom, but don't close the door just in case Angie gets an idea to grab ol' Trude and bolt. I splash some water on my face and take a good look in the mirror. One eye's black from a beat-down, the other junked up and sinking into my face as fast as the Lusitania. I feel my phone vibrate in my pocket, which has happened about ten times in the last five minutes. I need to puke again but decide to pull the phone out first and take a look. I've got five texts. Two are from Kyle, one is from Otto, one is from Liam, and one is from T-Mobile telling me my bill is due. I wish Teeny had just shot me.

I come out of the bathroom and Angie is sitting in a chair with her legs crossed, looking suddenly relaxed.

— I've just had a thought, tell me if you like it.

I already hate it but listen anyway.

— Let's go to the W, get a suite, and see how we feel about everything in a few hours.

— You going to soften me up with a little sex and room service?

— I wasn't thinking about sex, but they do make a wonderful tuna melt if you're up for guilty pleasures. We can even get a masseuse to come up to the room and exorcise of some of this darkness and distrust between us and then make a real decision about what to do.

I didn't know if she was looking out for me or still conning me, but the tuna melt sounded nice.

— What about Otto?

— What about him?

— You're just going to take his smock and give his priceless painting to some museum? You're shadier than I am.

— It's not his smock, it's Carla's.

— And what, you've decided she left it to you in her imaginary will?

— We discussed my buying it.

— When? Tearing down the 101 when you were getaway driving?

— She was my sister, Bobby, I think I know what she wanted, and she wouldn't have wanted Otto to have that smock, that I know. Now, can we *please* just get out of this horrible room?

— Fine, come on, I'll drop you at your car.

— You're not going to come to the hotel with me?

— Not right now.

She looks back down at the Klimt.

— I don't suppose you'd be willing to leave that in my care?

I didn't even bother answering.

43.

I come to pretzeled on the floor with my arm bent under me and the needle still in my thigh. I was trying to play it safe, so I just "muscled" it, but when you step back in the ring with the champ there's always a chance that you'll get knocked out. I pull out the point and push to a knee like an old palooka getting up off the canvas. I've been out for four hours and my arm's asleep. And I don't mean a few tingles, I mean like a frozen leg of lamb. This is how people die, first shot back after a layoff. It's a textbook story: out-of-work writer in recovery starts slinking around the old neighborhood, shooting up wayward brown girls, teaching his producer how to chase the dragon, searching the city for an ex-sponsee mixed up in dark affairs. He takes a toot off the foil in a moment of weakness, and before you know it he's in line at Walgreens buying a pack of syringes. He does a "safe shot" just to break the ice, and wakes up dead. Only I don't wake up dead. I wake up not dead. I'm a train, I'm a train, I'm a train, I'm a train, I'm a train, I'm a train.

I stumble to the bathroom and palm some water. My mouth's so dry my tongue hurts. I peek in the mirror. The eye's turned speckled purple. I look like a raccoon, and I feel like one shat in my head. I swing the dead arm. It's starting to thaw. If you jammed a fork into it, I might even feel it.

I probably should be thinking about the missing masterpiece I've got in my possession, the whereabouts of which would make the front page of every newspaper in the world but what's got my attention are three texts that just came in rapid succession from Andrew Wood. They read in order:

"There's news on the DreamWorks pitch."

"Call me or just come by."

"I'm at the office."

Otto and his Klimt may be hanging over my head like Damocles sword, but this is still LA, and when showbiz calls, everything else moves to the back burner.

#

— Hey Colleen, it's Bobby, is Andrew around?

— Oh, hi Bobby, let me see if I can get him off this call.

Wood's trio of texts are like a show business hieroglyphic, the meaning of which could be interpreted a hundred different ways. The part that's got my heart racing a little is the middle one which reads "call me or just come by." It's the "come by" part I'm reading into because producers don't like to deliver bad news ever, and sure as hell not in person, so if Wood is willing to have me in front of him, that could be good for the Jews, as they say. Now, as far as the first text goes, he just said "news on the DreamWorks pitch" not "good news" so that's tempering my hopes, but Wood has a flair for the dramatic, so he might want to deliver the good news to me directly. Then again, he might be so fucking gakked out on coke and God knows what that he hallucinated the whole thing.

— Dude, so glad you called, a lot going on.

He's "glad" I called. Please God, tell me they bought the fucking pitch.

— You got a minute?

— Yeah, I'm calling you, I got all the time you want. What's up?

— So much. So much. Did I tell you that I'm bidding on the life rights to Woody Woodpecker.

— You mean the guy who created it?

— No, Woody Woodpecker.

— The cartoon?

— No, Woody himself.

— But he's not a person, he's a drawing.

— Right, but I'm creating the mythology that he is a person and creating a legal paper trail along the way to prove it. I need to get the deal wrapped up because I'm going to detox sometime tonight.

— You're going to detox?

— Yeah, it's time.

It was time before he started smoking junk in my face, but I keep that to myself.

— Everyone thinks I'm going to Alabama to meet a surrogate about carrying a child for me, but I'm going to Panorama City.

— I know that place.

— Is it okay?

— Yeah. It's a detox.

— Hey look, would you mind if I put you down as my emergency contact? I can't have anyone I'm close to know what's going on.

— Sure, go ahead.

There was a long strange silence.

— So, you going to tell me what DreamWorks said?

— They're interested.

Thank you, God!

— But they don't like the father-son story.

— Okay, do they know what they want instead?

— They didn't say. They just want to buy the idea.

— What idea? The jukebox coming to life?

— No, the song-characters as characters in a movie, but maybe the jukebox too, though they think kids don't know what jukeboxes are and are wondering if it can be reimagined with Spotify.

— Sure. Not as historically iconic, but why not. They still want me to write it?

— No. They have another writer in mind.

The words hit me like the blast wave from an atomic bomb. I'm gutted. I think I may actually cry. But instead I just start laughing.

— I know, it's fucked.

— Who'd you talk to, Destitrino?

— He called this morning. Loved your pitch by the way, thought it was an old-fashioned movie, but in a good way.

— He loved it so much they want to hire another writer.

— I don't think it was him.

— It was Jeffrey?

— He didn't say.

— Well, if it wasn't the fat little frat boy, it was fucking Jeffrey, dude. Did you tell Oren?

— Not yet, but you should lose Oren. You're still a viable writer. You need a manager who understands your situation.

— What's my situation?

— You got some great credits from twenty years ago, and you need someone young and hungry to reintroduce you to this town.

— OK. You got someone in mind?

— No, but let me give it some thought.

— While you're banging your head against the wall in detox?

— Am I really going to be banging my head against the wall?

— No, they're going to have you loaded on Suboxone. But then you got to get off the Suboxone.

An awful silence fills the line. He's probably reading e-mails, as the debris of my career floats down all around me.

— Glad I didn't come all the way to the office to hear that news.

— So sorry how this went, dude.

He tries to strike a compassionate tone but can't pull it off.

— The movie business is dead. We remember when it wasn't, so we want to make like it's not, but it's a completely untenable model. There's just no longer a need for a communal viewing experience. I was reading this article where they were saying that over eighty percent of all media is being viewed on smartphones and that it's actually rewiring people's brains so that the laughter of others is now a signal of intrusion and danger as opposed to safety and affirmation.

— They're still making the movies you guys make, they're doing superheroes and animation.

— True, but they don't buy pitches.

— Then why were we working on one for three months?

— Because, that's what we do.

And as fucked-up as that sounded, he was absolutely right.

I fall back on my bed and let how big a mess I'd made of my life spread through my chest like a palm full of Vicks VapoRub.

— Hey bro, let me ask you something.

— Sure.

— You know any really wealthy, slightly shady art collectors?

— Maybe. Why?

I get ready to tell Wood the whole story, everything that's happened since Angie called, just like I'm pitching him a movie. It's a great tale and I know he'll love it, but as he just said, pitches are dead, especially for a gritty little noir where the hero wins by losing.

— Hey man, I got to go. Good luck at detox, my boy. You're gonna need it.

44.

It's not a studio, it's a bachelor, but it's on Seranno, so at least Lupita had that right. It's not a bad little crib if you're a nineteenth-century Russian novelist, a monk or a junkie, but a normal human being would lose their mind in a week. Kyle's high, but only like a car has gas in it to run. I, on the other hand, am completely off the reservation, using Katzenberg's rejection as inspiration to shoot a little ten cc speedball. There was hardly any coke in there, but it still did what injected cocaine does, which is howl through your ears like a freight train. While I was cooking it, Kyle said, "You do know you had endocarditis, right?" I answered, "I do," and that was that.

When I called him, I was ready for him to be really pissed, but his voice was soft and tender, like my stealing the key had brought us closer together. I guess betrayal is its own kind of intimacy, especially if you grew up mistaking it for love. I suggested I stop by. All he asked was that I pick up a pack of Q-tips because he was tired of using cigarette filters for cottons. As for the magic bag of art, I left that stuffed in my bedroom closet about a mile south and west of here, and though I told him about the smock, I didn't tell him about the Klimt. But I did bring along the Pee-Chee folder with the sketches, and he's been pouring over them for the last twenty minutes with a dazed expression.

— How'd you even meet her?

— We were copping from the same guy, seeing each other every day in the Ralph's parking lot. One day he didn't show up and I went over to her and said I could help her out.

— That's how all great romances start.

He didn't even smile. The sketches had him by the gills.

— Who were you meeting? Boris?

— Yeah.

— How'd she know him?

— How does anybody know anybody?

That one worked on a few levels. He put a cigarette to his mouth and his hand brushed over his chest like he was making sure his heart was still there.

— How'd you get these?

— You left them behind at the Snooty. They were in the lost and found.

I watch his eyebrows make sense of what I'd said.

— That's the folder I gave you your fourth step in.

— I know.

— You ever do it?

— No. You ever do yours?

— No. And look at us now ...

He didn't smile at that either and stared down at the drawings like he was ready to dive into them.

— She was something.

— You don't even know.

I did a little, but I still get a taste in my mouth like an envy-flavored cough drop.

— Those sketches are heartbreakers. You got a lot of talent, kid. When the lady down at the Snooty looked at those she said you must have really loved her.

— What lady?

— The housekeeper.

— She found her?

— No, but she talked to the one who did. She said she found her in the bathtub in her underwear and there was no water in it. She liked to fix in the tub?

He twitches at the question. I give him a moment to answer, but he doesn't.

— Those from that day?

He comes up off the pictures and looks at me.

— What do you want to know?

— Are those sketches from that day?

— Yeah.

— Did she always shoot up in the bathtub?

— Does it matter?

— Yes.

— Why?

— Because if you don't talk about that shit, it will haunt you. I mean it's going to haunt you anyway, but maybe a little less. Why was she in the bathtub?

— I put her there.

— To try and bring her back?

— Yeah. I was drawing her, and she asked me to go down to the store and get her a ginger ale and pack of smokes. I told her to just let me finish and I'd go in a minute, 'cause I was in a groove and what I was seeing was really getting onto the paper—

— Was that the half-finished one?

— Yeah, this one.

I got to my feet and came and looked over his shoulder. It was just a few lines, but it vibrated with the same innocence and heartache as the Klimt.

— Really gives you a feeling.

— I showed it to her, but she got all weird for some reason and wouldn't lie back down, so I just gave up and went to the store. I got stuck behind an argument between this old drunk and the Korean guy behind the register 'cause he wouldn't sell him a single cigarette so I had to go to another liquor store, and when I came back to the room she was out. I shook her and slapped her, but she was like a piece of wood. I was going to put her in the shower, but as soon as I picked her up, I knew.

— You call 911?

— No.

— Why?

— Would you call the police to the Snooty Fox with fresh tracks, a warrant out for a missed court appearance, and a white girl dead in the bathtub?

Point taken. I reached for the smokes on the milk crate, knocking one loose from the pack. I let my first exhale serve as a full measure rest.

— You think it was an accident, or had she just had enough?

It caught him by surprise and he actually thought about it.

— I don't know. Which is worse?

It was a good question, and I didn't have an answer. He grabbed for another smoke and sat back on a small sofa that had so many burn holes in it, it looked like the pattern of the material.

— I ran into this kid I went to fourth grade with when I was downtown. He's a lawyer, was wearing a suit, and started talking about how all these kids we went to school with are dead and that he had never had anyone really close to him die, and I was just thinking, I've had everyone who's really close to me die. A few of them right in front of me.

He stubs out his smoke like it's the last one he's ever going to have.

— Can I crash you with tonight, I'm feeling really squirrely, and I made an agreement with myself that when I get like this I'd try to be around sober people, just in case.

— I'm not sober.

— You're more sober than me.

At this point that was debatable.

— Dude, if you want to hurt yourself I'm not going to be able to stop you, and then it'll just have happened at my house, and I'll be left with all that.

He looks at me like he's an orphan, which he basically is.

— Please.

— Fine. But I got to go do some things. I might not be home for awhile.

— Can I come along?

— No.

— Okay.

But he stares at me like it's not okay.

— What?

— You're going to give me half of whatever you get for Carla's Matisse, right?

— I'm not selling it.

— Okay, well half of whatever you get for finding it or whatever.

— Let me see what happens. I'll take care of you, I promise.

— I don't want you to take care of me, I want half. And I should get more than half. If you want to know the truth I should get all of it.

I feel a gush of bile surge up from my gut, but even with a speedball in me I've enough AA in me to say:

— Okay, I'll keep that in mind.

I get up and head for the door.

— I'm serious man. She wanted me to have it. She told me. She wanted me to be okay.

— Understood.

— She loved me. We were together. She wanted me to move to Europe with her.

I reach for the knob.

— Just this one time, don't be a selfish asshole and do the right thing.

That one spins me around like a magnet.

— Kyle, you need to shut the fuck up and let me handle this and just be grateful that there is an actual person left in the world willing to have anything to do with your ridiculous, strung-out ass! I get it, okay, I fucking get it. The girl cared about you. You didn't care enough about her to call the paramedics when she OD'd, but you're ready to cash in on her smock. You're a fucking saint!

I thought he'd fight back, but his face went calm. Standing up for himself had been fun for a moment, but he was much more at home as a self-loathing junkie.

45.

The W in Westwood gets all the way Pershed-out at night, the tailored suits the business ladies wear at noon giving way to the slitted skirts and black shellac hair of slinked-out Iranian hotties.

I didn't give Angie any warning, I just texted from the lobby. She wrote back before I'd even finished. "Thank God you're here. Room 817, please hurry. I'm desperately worried about you." I interpreted that to mean please don't die until the art's in my hands.

The door opens, and she hugs me tight, and holds on, as if we've found each other again after a natural disaster. It turns into a tender kiss and then a less tender kiss and before you can say Diaghilev, the whole thing devolves into desperate mauling. She puts her hand on my belt but somehow I'm able to put a stop to it before we cross the demarcation line, though at this point there are no clear boundaries in any direction.

— You're not all that different on smack as you are off, are you?

The layman's always surprised when someone using isn't drooling on themselves in the corner.

— Strange how we've been thrown back together, isn't it, Bobby?

— We haven't been thrown anywhere. You called me on the phone.

— True, but it's strange how it's all played out. You have to admit that.

— Okay. If I have to.

— Are you upset with me?

— Why would I be upset with you? I was a broke out-of-work writer before, and I'm a broke out-of-work writer now. Only now I'm doing dope. Or smack, as you would say.

She crinkles her nose.

— Angie.

— Yes, sweetie.

I lowered my voice to a tender coo.

— I can't let you have the Klimt.

It wasn't what she wanted to hear.

— I'm going to take it back to Otto.

— That's a mistake, Bobby.

— Maybe, but that's what I need to do. Look, you know it exists now, and that he has it; you want him to do something noble with it you can work it out with him.

— He's not a noble person.

— Well, maybe you're noble enough for the both of you.

Her mouth goes tense and lipless.

— When were you thinking of going to Italy?

— I'm not sure.

— Is your friend there now?

— No, why do you ask?

— I want to go there.

— Yes, I said you could join me, and I meant it, but first we have to do the right thing by the Klimt.

— I don't want to go with you.

— What are you talking about?

I didn't answer quick enough so she kept talking.

— What, you want to go there by yourself? And what, write?

— No.

— Please don't tell me you want to go there with another woman.

— No! I want to go with Kyle! I want to take him there to kick.

— Well, get it out of your mind, because it's preposterous. Your friend Kyle should be in jail, not in a farmhouse in Tuscany!

— My friend Kyle was in love with your sister and she would want him to be okay.

— How do you know that?

— Because junkies want other junkies to get clean. Junkies want motherfuckers they *hate* to get clean, much less the people they really care about.

— She didn't care about him. He was just another lower companion.

— As opposed to classy types like Otto? You're incredible, you know that? That you could be that fucking clueless about what really goes on with addicts ... Fuck addicts, *human beings*. You think she liked guys like this director she was with, some guy with no idea what's really going on with her, hiring sober companions to chase her all over town, treating her like an exotic zoo animal he needs to rescue. All these dudes who have no idea what's it like to not be able to stop doing really bad shit to yourself. Look, I know you can't understand it, but there's something intensely real about being junkies together. Between the blood and the sex and the being sick and the getting well and spending every fucking minute together in this insane circumstance, it's as real as anything can be.

— So, I should pack him a lunch and send him off to Italy to get all better?

— Yes. That's exactly what you should do. But I'm not asking you to do it because it's right. I'm going to give you the smock.

— You're going to give me the Matisse?

— Yes.

— And what are you going to tell Otto?

— Don't worry about it. You just figure out what *you're* going to tell him, because he's going to know you got it.

She covered her nose with both hands like she was praying and went through a quick series of calculations in her mind.

— How long do you want to stay there?

— Italy? At least a month, and maybe up to three. How long is your friend in Japan?

— Six months. But you can't stay the whole six.

— Okay, fine, but I also want two round-trip tickets, and some money. Five thousand dollars now, and forty-five thousand more when I get back. Actually I might not want to have five thousand on me, I might want you to just wire me dough as we need it.

I waited for her to fight me on the money, but she didn't. The idea was getting real to her.

— You really think this is what Carla would have wanted?

— No, I think she would have wanted you to send us to Italy, and for Kyle to get the smock.

I saw a look come over her face. The look people get when they've just heard the truth and know it.

— And you're ready to give up three months of your life for this? What about your work?

— There is no work. There's just this.

— Just helping Kyle?

— Yes. And getting the fuck out of L.A. before I'm strung out too. If I don't, I'll be dead in a week.

— I could take you out of Los Angeles right now if you wanted. We could drive up the coast for a week or two and clear our heads and bloodstreams.

She opens her blue eyes wide to let me know the offer's real and I feel the sickening relief of another option.

— Angie.

My voice goes down to a loud whisper.

— I need to tell you something.

She gets the dread face.

— What?

— Carla asked me to go away with her and help her kick.

I promised myself I'd keep my mouth shut before I went up there but I knew I was going to tell her the second she opened the door.

— It was right near the end of our thing. We met for a coffee and she asked me to come down to the desert with her and dole out her meds and watch her for a few days.

Her mouth went from red to a bloodless blue.

— We made a plan to go that night. She was on her way to pick me up when I backed out.

She took a pause and her eyes softened.

— I know all this.

— She told you?

— She didn't have to. I was the one who suggested she reach out to you.

— You did?

She nodded.

— Why didn't you just tell me you wanted me to go with her?

— Because I thought if you knew you were doing it behind my back, you'd be more likely to say yes.

Always nice to find out what a high opinion the women you've dated have of you.

— Well, I didn't end up going.

— True, but not because of me ... I wish you had gone. It couldn't have turned out any worse than it has now.

I look down at the floor, feeling the hollow stupidity of sharing a big secret that turns out to not be a secret at all. Even worse it's a secret that's being kept from you. When I look up and Angie's staring at me with the British version of empathy.

— It's funny, isn't it?

— What is?

— That you got together with me when you have so much more in common with my sister.

Oh, it's funny alright. Funniest thing I've ever heard.

46.

I took Wilshire the whole way. From the garish five-million-dollar condos of the Wilshire Corridor, through the William Morris midnight of Beverly Hills. I held my nose through the Tar Pit stink of Miracle Mile, past the green neon ghost of the Gaylord Hotel. I kept to my task until the moonlit ponds of MacArthur Park were small in the rearview, and there was nothing left but the second-rate skyscrapers of Figueroa and Grand. One long asphalt scar containing the DNA of not just a city but a century. 15.3 miles worth and I didn't miss a light.

Otto's parked outside a gallery on Spring Street in a funky cream-colored '70s Rolls that looks yellow under the streetlamps. I had suggested we meet at The Prince, but he wasn't feeling it, and told me he was at an opening downtown, and to come there and we'd talk in the car. I should have just told him that the art was in the bag, and the bag was in my hands, so he'd be going wherever the fuck I wanted, but I wasn't looking to call the shots, I was looking to get out of L.A. with my limbs intact and my self-respect just a little bigger than my habit.

I hop out of the toy car and head up to his window. He's on the phone, and gestures for me to come around and get in with his big half-moon nailed hand.

— *Draüber haben wir nicht gesprochen ... Nein, nein, nein. Ich kann dich nicht in Big Sur treffen ... Mir ist es schiesse ich hasse natürliche Schönheit. Sie brauchen nicht Natura Schönheit zu malen.*

What a fucking language! It's bad enough being in a concentration camp but having to listen to that while you're there is beyond the pale.

— Inspiration *ist für Erfinder, nicht Künstler, Künstler müssen in einem Raum eingesperrt warden ...* Okay, okay, I will call you back. I cannot talk about this now.

He hangs up with a shake of his head.

— She is a sculptor. Possibly a good one. Works in neoprene rubber, what scuba divers wear. She can't decide if she wants to be colleagues or lovers. Zis is the problem with Berliners born after the wall came down. Zey cannot make up their minds about anything.

I smile like we're just two old pals shooting the shit.

— Nice ride. You got a good eye for beautiful British things.

— I bought it from Carla's father when he ran into trouble with za tax authority and had to sell everything. It vas in a garage outside London, but now I am a Californian, so I sent for it.

I got an image of him driving it up the PCH with a surfboard on the roof.

— So, screenwriter? *Vas ist los?*

I know enough Yiddish for that one.

— A lot. *Vas ist los* with you?

— A lot as well. Otto always has his spoon in many soups.

He swivels the big head and gives me the once-over.

— You look a little dull, screenwriter. Your violin player eyes are not quite as bright.

— Just been running around.

— No, I don't think so ...

He leans forward and gives me a knowing smirk.

— I think someone has been a verrrrry bad dog.

— I'm not high, man, trust me, I'm not going back there. I've just been running around handling things and not sleeping.

Injected Sodium Pentathol makes you tell the truth. Injected heroin makes you lie.

— Okay, we will call it a case of existential exhaustion.

— Call it whatever you want.

— Don't pout, screenwriter. I'm glad you can lie. Integrity is good for sure, but it is flexible like everything else.

The gospel according to Schlein.

— So, vhere is your friend? Don't get me wrong, I am beginning to enjoy your company, but I asked to talk to him.

— I talked to him for you.

— So you said in your text. And what did he say?

— Not that much. He's just trying to hang in there. He's pretty heartbroken.

— As am I.

— Yeah, well he seems a little more heartbroken than you.

— Come now, screenwriter, you are more sophisticated than this. His wound is fresh and shallow, so you are seeing it, mine is old and deep, so you are not. That is Carla's gift to us. She is *der Wundgeber.* The giver of wounds.

He wasn't wrong about that. I'd just met her once and she'd put a nice big gash in me.

— Did you talk with him about what we discussed?

— Yeah. He didn't know much. I mean he knew about the robe, and that you had it and she wanted it back, but he wasn't the one driving the car.

— That's what he told you?

— Yeah.

— Addicts are famous for lying, are they not?

— *I* wouldn't trust one.

— But you think he is telling the truth.

— I don't think anything. I just know it wasn't him.

— How do you know this?

— Because I know who it was.

This time the head didn't swivel, it snapped.

— Tell me, screenwriter. Who was it? Who was driving?

My mind blanks and I start scrambling. I probably should have thought about what I was going to say before I got in the car, but I've been playing it by ear my whole fucking life, so why stop now.

— You don't know him.

— Tell me, perhaps I do.

— You don't.

— Just tell me the name.

— His name's Boris.

Boris, forgive me, but Kyle put you in my head and you're the first name that came to mind.

— Boris what?

— I don't know. He's a dope dealer, a Bulgarian dude. He sells antique watches too, and he told Carla he could help her sell the smock. He's the one who drove her, Kyle didn't want to be involved.

— Well, vhere's the smock, does Boris have it?

— I don't know.

— What did Kyle say?

— Kyle doesn't know anything.

— You are lying.

— I'm not lying.

— And you are high now too. I have junkies chasing after junkies. Give me the number for this Bulgarian. I will handle it now.

— There's no need to talk to Boris.

— Give me his number, I am taking over.

— Dude, relax. I have it.

— So? Give it to me.

— No, not his number. I have *it*. The portrait of Trude Steiner. That freeze dried his whole fucking face.

— It's in my car.

— I don't believe you.

— Dude, are you kidding? How else would I know what it was? It was sealed up in ten rolls of duct tape, I have it. I have the Klimt.

I can see his mind working or not working. Whatever the case he knows I'm not lying.

— You are familiar with zis painting?

— I am now. I looked it up on the Internet. I'm not the only bad dog around here.

I said it in a way that told him he was safe, and his face relaxed a good three percent.

— You surprise me, screenwriter. I was only hoping that you would move the ball forward not score the goal.

— I just got lucky. Kyle didn't know anything, but some of the people he introduced to Carla did.

— Have any of them seen the painting?

— Nope, just me.

— Excellent. You've done well, screenwriter. I am going to take care of you.

— I don't need you to take care of me.

— Well, I am going to have to compensate you for your work.

— I don't want it. Just forget everything else.

— What do you mean?

— I mean I'm going to give you that painting, just that painting, that's it, I'm not going to ask you how you got it or what you're going to do with it or any of that, and you're going to forget about Matisse and everything else, especially me and Kyle.

— You want the smock as payment for the painting.

— I don't know anything about the smock, dude. I just want this over.

— Okay, screenwriter. I understand. That is acceptable to me.

— I'll bet it fucking is.

I reached for the door, the leather on the handle was as soft as the skin on Cupid's ass.

— Where are you going?

— To get the painting. That okay?

The fierce German eyes turned sheepish and just for a second "the

most interesting man in the world" felt like a fool. I got out, went
to the trunk of my car, unzipped the bag, took out the duct tape
mummy and threw it in a big canvas shopping bag. I got back in
the Rolls, pulled it out of the bag and handed it to him.

— Reach in there, so you know it's the thing.

He reached in and pulled out enough of the rolled canvas to see
the back of it in the yellow light.

— This is right.

He turned and placed it in the back seat.

— And here, take this too.

I went back to the bag and pulled the portfolio of Carla's pictures.

— What's zis?

— You've never seen it?

— No, What is it?

— Photographs. Go ahead, open it.

— I will open it later.

— Just open it.

He unzips the portfolio and looks at the first picture, the one with
the ball gag and lipstick across her chest.

— Art.

— Yeah, art.

I watch his eyes roll back when he comes to the milking stool. One
last wound from *der Wundgeber*.

47.

The sky is the color of a Camel smoker's lung as we cross Jefferson and head up that part of La Cienega that thinks it's a freeway. The Uber driver wanted to take the 101 to the 110 to the 105, but I don't believe in the 105, and told him it's La Cienega or bust.

Out my window, oil derricks are slowly rocking against burnt pink. Sometimes they look like skinny dinosaurs, sometimes like the giant hammers of a piano. If you quizzed a hundred Angelenos, not many could tell you that in 1890, L.A. was just a sleepy town of fifty thousand when some of the most productive oil fields in history were discovered out by Dodger Stadium, or that black crude was this city's first export thirty years before the world had ever heard of Rudolph Valentino.

Kyle's on the Baldwin Hills side, his terror pulling at us like a gravitational force. We spent the day getting our supplies together, making believe this was a well-thought-out plan, but we both know we're fleeing for our lives or maybe I just know it, and thank God I'm the one with the tickets.

— You all right?

He makes a noise and looks out the window.

— I haven't been on a plane since I was a kid.

— You serious?

— No, but it feels like it.

— I know what you mean.

And I do. Being strung out isn't conducive to air travel. Besides, the right mixture of dope and coke and you can pretty much go anywhere you want in your chair.

— What airline?

— Alitalia.

— You ever flown them before?

— I told you, I never been to Italy.

He nods, thinking about something else.

— You ever fly Lufthansa?

— No.

— El Al.

— No.

— KLM?

— What's that, Holland?

— I don't know. I just know it's an airline.

We take a right on La Tierja by Pann's Restaurant where a lot of people think *Pulp Fiction* was shot but wasn't.

— What about Aer Lingus, you ever fly Aer Lingus?

— All right, now you're crossing the line.

That gets a smile out of him, first one all day. He was excited about Tuscany at first but has been growing warier as the day's gone on. I actually put together a nice little detox kit for the boy and am acting like he's going to have a relatively soft landing, but we both know there are no soft landings and that eventually the gears are going to grind and grind hard. As for me, I'm telling myself I'm going to be fine once I clear city limits, but the truth is the fuse has been lit and there's a far better chance we end up with bloody arms in a Roman hotel room than there is of a successful kick under the Tuscan sun.

— It wasn't a liquor store.

— What wasn't?

He's back out the window, as we pass over the red taillights of the 405.

— Carla. I didn't go get her cigarettes.

I wait for him to keep going, but he doesn't.

— Where'd you go?

— I didn't go anywhere.

He pulls away from the window and stares into the driver's headrest.

— I'm not sure why, but she was in a really good mood. I had been drawing her for hours, the ones you found ... She was saying she wanted to show them to some people she knew, she thought they were really good.

He was talking to my knees, but it felt like he was looking right at me.

— We did a big shot, not huge, but big. She laid down on the bed and I started drawing again. Not what she looked like, who she was. Her aura, like I could see her under her skin, and I was like, oh shit, it's all just lines and light. Everything we see, it's all just lines and light. I went over to her and whispered how much I loved her in her ear and realized she wasn't breathing. I didn't know how long it had been. I was concentrating so hard on what I was doing, I didn't even realize what had happened.

An involuntary moan came out of me, not for Carla, but for Kyle.

— I need to burn those drawings.

— Kyle.

— I do, I need to burn those drawings.

— No, you don't. You need to get clean. You're still alive.

— I don't want to be.

— Bro, she was a dope fiend. An unbelievably compelling one, but a dope fiend, and dope fiends die, that's what they do. We just know a bunch who got clean, so we think *that's* normal but it's not normal. What's normal is they die.

— Well, maybe I should die.

— You're going to. Soon. Or even worse, you're going to live. Look, you've done it, okay ... everything there is to know about that life you know. How much more pain do you need? Besides, you're not the one who dies, the people you get high with do and you're left to carry it around. Look, don't make me do an AA speech. I'm so crazy right now I'm ready to have this guy turn left and take us right to Robert Lee's. Please. Let's just go to Tuscany and spend a month or two in the country being nice to ourselves, and if we decide we don't like it, we'll go to Rome and shoot dope and eat pasta 'til we're dead.

— I was looking right at her the whole time. The whole time.

48.

The flight attendants on Alitalia are very cinematic, and one brown-eyed Violetta has already Fellini'd her way into my heart. I may be high, hopeless and un-hirable, but I can still feel the hum of a nice-looking woman in a pair of pumps.

Somehow, we got through security without incident though my heart was in my throat when they took Kyle's bag off the conveyor belt and rummaged through. If he's got a loaded syringe it's up his ass, not in his knapsack. All detox meds are in my suitcase, save for a bar of Xanax, half of which I just washed down with tomato juice. I may not be as incorrigible as Colonel Strange, but I'm definitely guilty by disassociation.

I don't know if it's the big fluffy clouds, the blue kerchief Violetta has knotted around her neck or the fact that I found the Maltese Falcon and traded it in for two tickets to Rome and a villa with olive trees, but somehow the wind of hope is blowing through my nonexistent hair. I'm not even discouraged by the whole DreamWorks fiasco, and know in my soul that if I'm ever going to really make a comeback, it's going to be with a small, gritty personal tale that I make myself on a shoestring budget. I've even got my laptop out on the tray table and about to write FADE IN: on the script that changes everything. But I decide to jot a little note to Angie first:

"Hello "sweetie." I'm fifty thousand feet over Omaha and feeling no pain, except maybe a little twinge about you. Clearly, I'm a troubled boy, since all you did was lie to me and use me for my vast network of drug-addled connections, but somehow, whatever it was that makes whatever we have whatever, it is still got to me in some way. You once told me "The whole point of sex is to make two people feel closer than they really are." First off, I wish *I* had said that, and second off I think you're absolutely right, but hey, there are worse delusions to be under. Jesus Christ, I just realized how badly you must have wanted that smock to actually allow two crazed dope fiends to use your friend's rustic palazzo as a rehab. That being said, I'll try to keep whatever fluids Kyle produces in one room and promise that if one or both of us can't make it, we will head to the city and not stain the olive trees with blood. I can't really tell you why, but for some reason I'm hopeful. There's a saying in the program that goes, "Sobriety's not for people who need it, it's for people who want it," but it's not for either. It's for people who are somehow lucky enough to get it. I'm sorry your sister wasn't one of them. Anyway, that's what I got for now. I know we don't really know what to do with each other and never have, but we sure have packed a lot of story into a short period of time, and in my book, story's worth a lot. A whole lot."

I'm about to sign it "Zorn" when I feel a commotion behind me and see Violetta whiz by with quick narrow steps. I turn around, a few passengers and a male flight attendant are clumped outside the bathrooms. Violetta rushes toward them as the flight attendant leans toward her with urgency, talking over an old Italian woman's head. A wave of doom washes over me, not because I'm scared the plane's going to crash, but because Kyle went to the bathroom when I started writing Angie and he hasn't come back. I dump my open computer in his empty seat, close the tray table, and rush to the back. Violetta sees me coming and as I get close she says in her charming accent:

— Your friend has been in the bathroom for thirty minutes and he is not responding to our knocking. Maybe he is sick?

Oh no. I squeeze by her and knock on the door.

— Kyle ... Kyle, it's me.

Nothing. I knock loudly, startling the entire back of the plane, and scream:

— Kyle!

Fuck! I turn to Violetta.

— Can you get the door open?

— Yes, but—

— Do it.

She looks to her colleague.

— Just open the door!

He nods at her, and Violetta flips up the little sign that says lavatory, then slides a lever that turns the red "occupied" sign to green. I push open the door and there's Kyle, doubled over on the toilet. I lunge for him and get to work.

Tommy Swerdlow, born 1962, is an American actor and screenwriter. He has appeared in such films as *Howard the Duck* (1986) and *Spaceballs* (1987) and co-wrote the screenplays of *Cool Runnings* (1993), *Little Giants* (1994), *Snow Dogs* (2002) and *The Grinch* (2018). Swerdlow made his directorial debut with the 2017 feature *A Thousand Junkies*.